Laredo Gold

Wade Tulane had a secret to hide as he rode towards Laredo, but his immediate concern was for a young lad who was obviously badly wounded yet refused help. The pair met later in town when Wade discovered that the boy was Tommy Camden. He and his sister Stella were trying to find evidence to bring their father's killer to justice.

Now Wade had bought into their fight and it wasn't long before he had made deadly enemies in the town. His life was on the line and only his remarkable skills with gun and fist could save him long enough to uncover the mysteries which had brought tragedy and death to Laredo.

Laredo Gold

PETER WEBB

A Black Horse Western

ROBERT HALE · LONDON

© 1956, 2002 Norman Lazenby
First hardcover edition 2002
Originally published in paperback as
Double X Ranch by W.B. Glaston

ISBN 0 7090 7183 3

Robert Hale Limited
Clerkenwell House
Clerkenwell Green
London EC1R 0HT

*All characters in this story are entirely fictitious
and have no relation to any living person*

Typeset by
Derek Doyle & Associates, Liverpool.
Printed and bound in Great Britain by
Antony Rowe Limited, Wiltshire.

1

TRAIL TO TROUBLE

He rode up out of the desert, a tall grim man stooped in the saddle, on a trail-tired horse. Dust coated his Stetson and caked with the sweat on his red kerchief around his neck. His black shirt had its quota of dust and sweat from the desert ride.

At a touch of the reins, the black horse paused on the shale ridge. Wade Tulane stared across the heat hazes to the toy-like spread of buildings that marked the outskirts of Laredo. With tired fingers, he fumbled for the makings and began to shape a brown-paper cigarette.

Laredo! It was the name of a boom-town. Down here in Texas, close to the Mexican border, men and money swirled around cattle, the newly-opened railroad and the newly-discovered gold. The combination attracted the hardy and the greedy, and men like Wade Tulane.

He nudged his horse into the slow plodding stride which the animal could maintain all day if needed. It was tired, sweat-flecked and smelled of hot saddle-leather. They went down the shale slope to the sandy bed of the gully. Heat rose from the earth like an oven blast. Silvery cholla cactus, miraculously extracting moisture from roots deep in soil, filled rocky clefts. Away to his right, two gaunt Joshua trees stood like sentinels.

Wade hunched in the saddle and brooded, content to allow the passage of time to bring him into Laredo. In any case, the black horse could not be hurried. His dark eyes assumed a reflective gleam as he thought: 'Laredo might be the place for me . . . at least it's a long way from Colorado. Might be a place for a man to stop. . .'

The cayuse moved slowly; came out of the gully and plodded over the sand and shale. After half-a-mile they rounded a straggle of rocky outcrops lying on the desert as if thrown by a giant hand.

Wade Tulane sighted the other rider coming around the outcrop and his eyes narrowed and his lips became a tight firm line. He had a natural poker-face, with a taut mouth that revealed his iron character.

The stranger was badly wounded – that much Wade saw in a glance. He rolled in the saddle, holding the rawhide ribbons with one hand while the other clutched a red patch on his left shoulder. He was urging his bronc along the narrow trail between rocks when, surprised, he sighted Wade. He made to force his way past Wade's horse, but a hand went out and grabbed the animal's headstall and brought the horse to a halt.

'Let me git past!' The wounded person was young, with the shrill voice of a boy in his late teens.

'How come yuh're hit?' Wade continued to hold the horse. With a sharp glance, he noted the Colt in the stiff, new leather holster. 'Yuh got into a bit trouble?'

'Let me ride on!' snapped the other.

Again he tried to urge his bronc on but Wade kept the animal's head down. The horse jibbed restlessly under the treatment.

'Yuh'll be durned lucky if yuh reach town without fallin' off thet hoss!' rapped Wade. 'Let me help yuh, amigo!'

'Doggone it – let me git away!' shrilled the young man. 'I can look after myself. I ain't hurt so badly. It – it – was just an accident. A gun went off.'

Wade Tulane narrowed his eyes. He knew when a person was lying, for long experience in encountering strangers on lonesome trails had made him shrewd. And this boy did not lie very well. Wade figured the youngster had got his wound in anything but an accident.

7

He released the headstall of the other horse. The young lad jabbed spur rowels to flanks and the animal sprang away. Wade sat tall in the saddle and watched the young fellow ride away as quickly as possible for one in his wounded condition.

Wade rubbed a hand over his bristly chin and ruminated. 'Wal, ain't my grief. Obstinate young colt, anyways!'

He rode into Laredo some time later and his first thought was for his trail-tired black horse. He found a livery and led the animal inside, removed the saddle, blanket and headstall and then handed over to the wrangler with instruction to rub down, water and feed the horse. Then Wade Tulane walked out into the dusty street and stared at the nearest hotel. It was called the Bonanza Hotel, and the big two-storey place with ornate façade looked just what he needed. Inside he would find rest, food and drink and maybe a game of faro, for Wade was no saint and lived hard at times.

He walked stiffly into the hotel, carrying his saddlegear and small canvas poke which contained his few worldly possessions such as a change of shirt and socks.

He pushed through the batwing doors; stared around the sparsely patronised bar-room and then approached a small desk which was there for the convenience of visitors who wanted more than just a slug of whisky. There was no one at the desk. Wade waited a few seconds and then thumped tiredly on the polished pine.

A thick-set man, looking hot in a black suit and black silk necktie, came up to the wanderer.

'Anythin' I can do for you, stranger?'

Wade turned slowly. 'Yep. I want a room an' hot water brought up an' some place to dump this gear.'

'You can do that in your room,' said the other curtly. 'Follow me, Mister —?'

'Wade Tulane.' The trail-tired man searched the hotel manager's face. There was no real reason why the name should mean anything to a hotel-keeper in Laredo, but one never knew. News sure travelled strangely, and maybe there were Clorado men in this corner of Texas.

'I'll show you a room, Mister Tulane,' said the manager abruptly. He glanced at Wade. 'You sure need a wash-up. You've been ridin' all day, I guess.' He altered his tone grimly. 'Keep those hoglegs in the leather, Mister Tulane. Naturally, I don't like gun-play in this hotel.'

Wade nodded curtly. 'Sure. Let's go. I'm blamed tired and I hanker for that wash-up.'

They walked up creaking stairs to a wide landing and from there Wade Tulane was shown a room. Ten minutes later a two-gallon jug of steaming water was brought up to him by a whiskered old-timer who was apparently acting as waiter. The oldster shuffled into the room and set the big jug down on the wash-stand and then turned to Wade. It was a signal for both men to give way to astonishment.

'Ezra Sloan! Yuh old galoot!'

'Migosh – Wade Tulane hisself!'

Wade's smile faded as fast as it had arrived.

'You been workin' here long, Ezra?'

'Jest about two months,' grinned the other.

'You git tired of Cactus Plain up in Colorado?'

'I allus was a wanderer,' cackled the oldster. 'I jest figured I'd been around Cactus Plain too durned long.

'Wal; how come you're down this away? Last time I saw yuh it was at a placer claim an' yuh had a pardner. Yuh sure seemed to be doin' all right.'

Wade turned to the wash-stand. 'It petered out. I got sick of Colorado an' rode out. Guess I jest kept on movin' and now I'm here.'

'Yeah? Why in heck didn't yuh pardner a-come with yuh, Wade?'

Wade half-turned a grim face to the oldster. 'Jack Rawkin is dead – got himself killed.'

'A Colt slug?'

'Yep.'

Ezra Sloan scratched his grizzled old head. 'Wal, as I remember, Jack Rawkin was a healthy galoot. Only thing thet could ha' sent a feller like that to Boot Hill would be a slug. Who killed him?'

Wade Tulane poured some water out of the steaming jug before replying. 'He got bushwhacked. Nobody knows who killed him. Jest forget about it, will yuh?' Ezra blinked and then fumbled for a chew of tobacco, which he brought out of his flapping old vest.

'Sure, if yuh don't want to think about it, I'll fergit it. Reckon it ain't so good to lose a pardner. Say, yuh aim to look fer gold around these parts?'

'Maybe. I'm in no hurry to look for anythin'. And right now, Ezra, I'd be mighty pleased if you'd mosey along and let a man wash-up an' shave.'

The oldster cackled. 'Heh! Heh! Reckon I talk too much. I'll see yuh again. Iffen yuh want a pardner to look fer gold, remember I know more about placer claims than some of these jumped-up *hombres* that's hellin' into Laredo in the hope of findin' the stuff. Reckon I'm a mighty fit *hombre*, an' too young to waste my time as a hotel swamper. I —'

'Hell, Ezra – git!'

The oldster gave a cackling laugh and disappeared through the open door.

Wade Tulane gave his attention to his wash-up. There was a luxury in hot water and soap that only those who had travelled a long trail could appreciate. He stripped down to the waist and washed. Then he shaved, using the long-handled razor he took from his canvas poke. He was tired, coldly-grim inside and

11

he went on with the cleaning up process from sheer deliberation. He was not a range tramp, although he had acquired the appearance of one these past few weeks.

Eventually, he washed all over, getting rid of the dust and sweat. He beat the dust out of his brown trousers and climbed back into them because that was all he possessed. He got a clean shirt out of his poke and donned it. He polished his boots; beat dust out of his Stetson. He buckled his cartridge belt on to the familiar notch; it kept up his pants! Then the gun-belt went on. The two Colts lay fairly high, on his hips, because Wade Tulane was a long-bodied man and had long arms. He could reach the six-shooters just nicely. Not for him the low-slung gun that rested almost on a man's thigh.

He went out of his room some time later and locked the door behind him. Ezra Sloan could take the used water away some other time. He locked the door because he didn't want snoopers rummaging through the few belongings he had in the canvas saddle-bag.

Wade Tulane went down to the bar of the Bonanza Hotel and drank a quick shot of the Laredo version of red-eye. It put some immediate energy into him. But he knew a much better idea would be to take in some real grub.

He went out for that. The Bonanza Hotel seemed

slow and any grub he asked for would have to be specially prepared.

He went along the boardwalk until he hit a Chinese restaurant and, turning through the batwings, he walked into a satisfying atmosphere of hot cooking.

He got what he needed to satisfy the inner man in the shape of jerky beef and gravy and beans followed by apple tart and sauce. He drank from a big cup of coffee while eating. He didn't give much attention to the other customers but knew there were noisy cowpokes, miners and railroad workers in the eating-house. They were just a background.

He left the restaurant some time later and stood on the boardwalk and scanned the activities of Laredo. The dusty street bore a slow-plodding mule train – six of the critters hauling a huge wagon. A Concord stage was outside a freight office being loaded with passengers' baggage. A prospector led a burro around a corner and stopped at the assayer's office. Wade heard the tinkle of a piano from a saloon called 'La Belle' which lay on a corner of the square formed in the centre of the town. The heat of the sun was everywhere. In an alley across the main stem, Mexican children and some dogs played in the alkali dust.

It was a familiar enough scene to Wade Tulane. Most cow-towns followed a pattern. Yet he knew that Laredo was bursting at the seams with varying activities, and at night there would be a roaring assembly of the goldminers, the cow-men and the railroad workers.

He wandered along the boardwalk, smoking a cigarette of his own making. He paused and stared into a store window and viewed with interest a new-fangled idea in the shape of peaches in a can! Then there were cigarettes, already made-up, in packets. What next would they think of?

Wade was passing a clothing emporium when the door suddenly opened with the jangling of a bell and a young man stepped out on to the boardwalk. He halted as he stared at Wade Tulane. In fact, the surprise was mutual.

The young fellow obviously had a bandage under his red shirt. Wade could see a bit of it, and the youngster was carrying his left arm stiffly. He was a slender lad with fair hair and probably not even eighteen. After his first start of surprise, he tried to slip past Wade Tulane but was obstructed by an iron arm.

'Git out o' my way, stranger!'

'Did yuh leave a dead man out thar in the desert by any chance?' drawled Wade. 'Somebody shot yuh so what happened to the *hombre* who did the shootin'? He git away – or what?'

'Why can't yuh mind yore own business?' snapped the young fellow.

'Yep, maybe yuh're right,' admitted Wade. He

lowered his arm. 'Jest lettin' curiosity git the better o' me, that's all. Wal —.'

The emporium door-bell jangled again and suddenly, it seemed, a girl was revealed standing in the open space. Wade stared at fair hair and a clear oval face. Her hair was twisted around in an ornate bun at the back of her head – that much he saw as she looked sharply at the young fellow and himself. She wore a simple gingham dress in green and white checks and Wade was conscious of a womanly body although she could not have been more than a few years older than the young *hombre*.

An instant thought came to him: these two were brother and sister. It was just a hunch he had.

'Why are you stopping him?' cried the girl. 'I saw you through the window!'

Wade Tulane gave that slow crooked grin of his. He didn't realise it, but it lent a handsome twist to his taut, wary face.

'Ain't nothing much, ma'am. Jest happens I saw this young feller when I was ridin' into town earlier this day and I noted he had stopped a slug. I figured to help him, but he fed steel to his hoss and rode away. Shore is a wonder to me he made it into town. Guess he must be hardy, huh?'

The girl held his glance for a moment and then lowered long-lashed eyes.

'Tommy had – an – an – accident. He's all right

now. Thank – thank – you for thinking of helping him.'

'I'm a-going, Stella,' muttered the young man. 'Don't worry about me – an' tell this stranger we don't need any help.'

With that he walked away quickly along the board-walk and, reaching a tie-rail, gathered the ribbons of a bronc and leaped neatly to the saddle and rode off.

With a slow smile, Wade took off his hat and looked at the girl. 'Yuh patch him up or did a Doc do it?' Grey eyes flicked him momentarily.

'A doctor attended to Tommy, thank you.'

'Your brother?'

'Yes.' She gave a slight smile. 'You guessed that!'

Wade Tulane flicked a glance at the gold lettering on the central window-pane of the store. He saw the legend: W. CAMDEN. Draper.

'Thet can't be you.' He nodded at the sign. 'Maybe yuh work here?'

'W. Camden was my father,' said the girl clearly. 'He's dead – only a few weeks ago. Anyone in Laredo could have told you that.'

Wade Tulane replaced his hat; slid the thong tight under his chin. 'Sorry to hear thet, ma'am. In thet case yuh ought to look after yore brother. Thet slug in his shoulder could easily ha' been nearer the heart.'

'Oh, I know that —' She stopped and looked

confused.

'Yuh want any help?' asked Wade quietly.

'I – I – I've got friends!'

'Shore. Reckon a gal as pretty as yuh will have friends.' Wade made a swift gesture to his guns. 'These are my only friends, ma'am. My name is Wade Tulane. I've just ridden into this town an' I'm right now at the Bonanza Hotel. Thet offer of help still stands.'

She looked at him uncertainly. He knew what she was thinking. He was a stranger in a town of hard characters, and he was rough and he carried two guns.

Wade grinned, and he little realized how it wiped away the wary imprint on his face.

'I'll know where to find you!' gasped the girl, and she turned and ran into the shop.

Wade strode away and grinned at the boardwalk. He wondered if his offer to help the girl had been a wise one. Maybe he should be minding his own business in this town.

Maybe he had got the wrong impression from Tommy Camden's remark about not needing help from any stranger.

Still, he had the feeling the two had a bit of trouble on their hands, but what it was he could not hazard a guess.

Wade Tulane reached the Bonanza Hotel and

entered the lounge. He slumped down in a leather chair, feeling bone-tired with the ride he had started that day long before sun-up. The lassitude that comes to any man after a hearty meal hit him. He reached out for a newspaper that was lying on a nearby table and scanned it. The sheet was headed: *Laredo Journal.* The long columns of print were slightly imperfect, but Wade did not notice that. He slumped further in the easy chair and felt he could quite easily go to sleep. He let the sheet drop to one side.

He came to instant alertness some ten minutes later when bawling voices arose in the air from outside the hotel. He knew it for a fight from the first moment. Out of curiosity, he went to the window and looked out.

Two men were slugging at each other and onlookers were already forming a circle around them. Shouts and jeers went up in the air. Wade saw a youngish man in the black suit usually favoured by gamblers, doctors and mayors. He got a sudden hunch that this man was a gambler. He was opposed by another man who seemed a good fifteen years older, if iron-grey hair and a heavier body were any guide.

Hats lay in the dust. One black hat and one Stetson. Wade saw the older man shrug out of his coat and hand it to someone in the crowd. Then the young gambler whipped out of his black coat and rushed in to renew the fight. Punches were slung as the men faced up to each other in the style of the times.

Wade smiled slightly and figured he might as well get a closer view. He liked a good fight as well as the next man.

He walked out of the hotel and crossed the board-walk. He joined the circle of grinning and cheering onlookers. Somehow, within seconds, he found himself on the inside of the ring. The onlookers were eddying around so much that he didn't have to push forward.

The young gambler with the white vicious face was suddenly getting the worst of the brawl. Wade saw that and gave a shrewd glance at the older man. He figured him for a rancher. There was that solid look of the steady-going man.

The fight was suddenly going bad for the young gambler for he took plenty of slamming blows to the body and face. Jeers and shouts went up from the crowd, but Wade Tulane could discover no reason for the fight. But reason there must be. Probably some old hatred.

The younger man crashed to the dusty road and lay glaring. Then he scrambled up again and rushed forward.

Wade saw the man's hand flash to his armpit. He

knew in an instant what was hidden under that fancy vest.

The small Derringer flashed out the next second and pointed across the intervening space at the other man. Wade had seen these shoulder guns. It was a typical gambler's idea. Usually a gambler paraded the fact that he wore no Colts, but some were known to carry hidden Derringers.

As the small gun gleamed in the man's hand, Wade Tulane drew a Colt. It was one of his fastest draws. His .45 exploded possibly a split-second before the Derringer barked, but no one could have described it. The gambler's gun seemed to crack and then leap from his hand. Like a firework, it jerked a few yards to one side, leaving the man staring at his numbed hand.

The shouts died away. The onlookers turned heads almost simultaneously to stare at Wade Tulane. The tableau held for what seemed a long time, but it was only seconds.

'Reckon thet was a pesky trick – tryin' to shoot a man in the middle of a fight!' drawled Wade, and he glanced around warily. 'Shore hope yuh fellers figure it that way, too!'

A chorus of growls seemed to signify general assent, and the crowd began to break up, conscious that the fight was over. Wade watched the young gambler take his black coat from a pal in the crowd and then bend down and pick up his small gun. The man walked close to Wade Tulane. Eyes glittered in a pale face as he sneered: 'I'll remember yuh!'

Wade slowly holstered his Colt, without looking down. He stood and waited. He hardly wanted to turn his back and invite trouble. The young gambler had pals in the crowd, it seemed.

The other man walked up to Wade and stuck out a hand in friendship.

'Thanks. Yuh mebbe saved my life. Dave Latimer is the name.'

'Think nothin' of it.' Wade smiled as he took the other's grip. He watched as a friend of Dave Latimer's helped him on with his brown coat and then handed him his gun-belt, which he strapped on. Not until this was done was there anything said. Then: 'That Leo Sand is a durned hellion. But I figure I could ha' licked him.'

'What was the trouble?'

'I warned him to keep away from a young gal called Stella Camden. He's pesterin' her to marry him!'

2

THE SKUNK

Wade Tulane moved slowly around on his heel. 'I've met Miss Camden.'

Surprise showed in Dave Latimer's face. 'Yuh have? I thought I knew all her friends. I'm by way of bein' her guardian since her father died.'

Understanding of the cause of the fight came to Wade. He nodded.

'I met Tommy Camden out in the desert,' he said slowly. 'He was wounded an' I figured he might fall off his hoss – but seems like he's a hardy lad and made it back to town. Then I met up with him again beside the draper's store, and Miss Stella came out. Ain't none of my bizness, but I got a feelin' those two have some grief on their hands.'

A frown crossed Dave Latimer's honest face. His shrewd eyes appraised Wade Tulane; dropped down to the two Colts slung in the gun-belt. A stranger, he

23

decided, and Laredo was full of them. But this man had saved his life.

'William Camden, their father, was killed by a bushwhack slug,' he said. 'He was a great feller and a firm believer in the future of this town. He didn't like the rabble that has poured into the burg but he always hoped that the discovery of gold would bring progress to the town and not just trouble. Then he was found in a canyon some seven miles east of the town. There was a rifle bullet in his back. William Camden didn't tote a gun of any sort – never did. He called himself a trader and was agin guns. I figure it kinda ironical that he should die that way.'

'Who the hell would kill a gent like that?'

'The sheriff never found a durned thing. Guess it is a complete blank. Nobody knows who killed him – 'cept the killer. And we never figured out why William was ridin' out through that canyon. He was mostly a townsman. Never went far.'

'Guess all that is worryin' Stella and Tommy,' said Wade. 'Still ain't none o' my bizness – but one last question: you got any idee who Tommy Camden has tangled with to git thet slug in his shoulder?'

Dave Latimer frowned again. 'That I don't know. Mebbe I ought to talk to that younker.'

Wade branched off on another kind of question. 'What's wrong with Leo Sand apart from him bein' a gambler?'

'Wrong!' exploded the other. 'That jasper is all wrong for anybody, never mind a young gal who can have her choice of *hombres* in this town! Leo Sand is a skunk! Yes, sir! For a start, he won't work an' he drinks an' gambles – usually to win, I'll allow! Aw, shucks, I've told him to keep away from Stella. For some durned reason he's been pestering her to marry him at every chance he gits. Marry that waster! I'll nail his hide to a barn-door!'

Dave Latimer's indignation caused Wade to smile thinly.

'Yuh a rancher?' he asked.

'Yep. Own the Cloverleaf down the valley. Ever yuh ride that way yuh'll be welcome to hitch up for the night.'

'I'm Wade Tulane – bit of a wanderer, I guess. I might try workin' a claim on the River Shasta – if I kin find anythin' to claim.'

The other laughed. 'Those placer miners are shore diggin' lumps out o' that river. But the quartz is bein' mined in the hills – only yuh need machinery for that. Say, if yuh want a job mebbe I could fix yuh up if yuh can ride herd.'

'I'll think about it, Mister Latimer.'

The other laughed. 'Call me Dave next time yuh see me!'

They parted, Wade Tulane entering his hotel again and the rancher going his way. Wade thought

25

he would stand a better chance of a rest if he went up to his room and stretched out on the bed. If a man had any sense, he took his rest when he could get it.

He eased off his boots and unbuckled his belt and looped it over the brass rail at the head of the bed. It sure seemed a long time since he had used a bed.

He lay back and stared at the huge decorations that constituted the pattern of the wall-paper. He was thinking of Jack Rawkin in no time. And it was all wrong because he could only think about his dead partner with grim distaste and bitter feelings.

It was because of Jack Rawkin's death he was riding the trails, a fugitive from Colorado. Maybe even now Wanted posters were being delivered to sheriffs over a wide area. Maybe the sheriff's office in Laredo had one. He would have to find out.

Wade shut his eyes; took in a deep breath. He didn't go to sleep at once although he was bone-tired. Nope. Instead he had a vision of Jack Rawkin as he had last seen him – the galoot loading the saddle-bags of his horse with the little leather sacks of gold dust – working furiously to load up – before his partner arrived back – the tent at one side of the camp – the river not far away – and Jack Rawkin going for his gun – desperately surprised at the unexpected return of his partner from the nearby town of Cactus Plain.

Jack Rawkin had lost on the gun-play, that was all. He had fallen to the ground, dead. The gold for which he had attempted to double-cross his partner had stayed in the saddle-bags. And the horse, spooked by the sudden shots, had dashed off.

Wade Tulane had ridden after the cayuse, naturally. And he had had the devil's own luck to encounter the sheriff's posse as they rode out on some other business.

Wade had turned his horse on the impulse and Jack Rawkin's animal had ran on, carrying the hard-won gold away.

Only minutes later and there had been no time for explanations. The sheriff had discovered the body of Jack Rawkin and thought the worst. It looked like a clear case of murder, the old story of killing to secure a double share of gold. The sheriff, raging over other lawlessness, had sent the posse chasing after Wade Tulane. And Wade had been foolish enough to rowel his nag instead of staying to explain.

That was all it was. He had kept on riding. As the days passed and he crossed the State-line, he knew his chances of being believed were fading for ever. The older the case, the less chance there was of the set-up being believed.

Wade groaned. So there would be Wanted posters outside lawmen's offices. The best he could hope for was that the affair would some day be lost and forgotten among the rest of the unpunished violences of the West.

He had told Ezra Sloan the first yarn that had entered his mind. There was only one trouble: so far Ezra was the only one in Laredo who could connect him with Jack Rawkin.

Wade Tulane gradually relaxed on the bed and sleep took over. But it was the type of sleep from which he could awaken in an instant. He could be alert, a wary man with guns in his hands at a second's warning. But nothing disturbed him and the sun sank lower outside. The time came when it shot crimson claws into the sky from its position on the horizon.

At night he went down into the bar-room and stood against the polished counter. The place was filling up. There were groups of punchers, groups of miners and the Irishmen from the railroad. Card games were in progress and, staring over the haze of smoke, Wade saw Leo Sand at a table with three other men who, by their garb, seemed to be cowpokes.

Wade turned back to his Hermosilla beer. That Leo Sand should use the Bonanza Hotel as a place for his gambling was none of his business.

But the young gambler seemed bent on making himself unpleasant. As soon as he caught sight of Wade at the bar, he finished a hand and then stood up with a muttered few words, to his companions. He strode over slowly, soft leather boots making his approach stealthy. Wade noticed him almost at once and turned casually.

Wade's dark eyes flicked the other's white face. He waited, thumbs hitched in his belt. He had not long to wait.

'I didn't like yore play this afternoon,' said Leo Sand softly. 'You damned near shot a bit out o' my hand.'

Wade could have ignored the statement of something which was now past and done. But he thought a warning should be handed this galoot.

'Lay off me, Mister. I carry two guns and they've been used.' It was a clipped warning, uttered so low that only the gambler could hear.

'I'm rememberin' you.' Leo Sand's tone was sibilant. There was nothing idle in his threat. His white face was taut with anger.

'Shore, you remember,' snapped Wade. 'Yuh jest remember, pal, thet I got two hoglegs an' I ain't the type to bushwhack easily!'

Wade dropped his gaze momentarily. Sure enough, Leo Sand did not wear any guns that were visible. But it was a good bet that his shoulder-holster was filled. Wade glanced at the fancy vest and grinned.

'Why don't yuh button up, amigo?'

And with slow but steady movements he reached out and twisted the two top buttons of the vest into their respective buttonholes. Leo Sand fumed for the few seconds and then his hand whipped up and gripped Wade's.

'Cut it out!' Fury made his lower lip tremble.

'Sure!' drawled Wade, and he straightened back to the counter. But his gaze never deviated from the other's glittering eyes.

Without another word, Leo Sand spun around and walked back to the card table.

Wade figured he had made an enemy. It wasn't funny. With a short laugh, he turned to his beer. Few in the bar-room had seen the incident; most of the men were arguing and confabbing loudly.

There was one thing he knew; Leo Sand was not the type who wanted to stage a gun-fight on the basis of the fastest draw. But his quickly-formed hatred of Wade Tulane was very real. It might provoke him into a sly shot in a dark alley.

Wade thought the bar-room of the Bonanza Hotel was a bit confining after the annoying interlude so he walked out.

As he pushed through the doors, he did not see the bitter glance Leo Sand arrowed after him.

Wade went along the boardwalk, a big wary man in a dark shirt that stretched tight across a wide chest. His boots clomped regularly on the boardwalk. He went on steadily but he had no real destination until, suddenly, and to his surprise, he was outside the little drapery store.

He halted. He was all at once undecided. It was a novel experience for a man who usually went ahead rightly or wrongly on any project that was his concern.

He rolled a cigarette and lit it with a sulphur match. He stared at the glimmer of light that showed from somewhere beyond the street-window of the store. The front door seemed shut. But maybe she would open up if he knocked.

'Aw, shucks!' he muttered. 'Who says thet gal wants to be bothered with the likes o' me!'

As he hardly knew his own mind, there was no answer to this question.

His wary eyes suddenly saw a burly man walking across the road. Yellow light from a nearby saloon showed the star pinned to the galoot's long-tailed coat. Looked like the sheriff. Deputies were usually content to dispense with the wearing of a coat.

Wade instinctively tensed and then he relaxed with a bitter smile as the other man mounted the boardwalk. In the half-light the other could not have seen him properly so it did not seem that the sheriff was coming over to meet up with him.

But the man came quite close. Before he halted outside the door of the drapery emporium, he flashed a glance at Wade. Then, looking away again, the sheriff knocked on the door. Wade kept on propping up the wall. He was close enough to see the features of the sheriff even in the half-light.

Then the store door opened and a shaft of lamp-light fell out over the boardwalk. Wade got a swift impression of Stella Camden's dismayed face and the stern look on the heavy features of the sheriff, and then he heard talk.

'I don't like to do this, Miss Stella, but I got to see thet brother o' yore's. Reckon he's at home, huh?'

'I – I – why – why do you want him, Sheriff Hapner?'

'Yuh ought to know, Miss Stella,' said the sheriff flatly. 'He's been in a shootin' affair an' what's more the body of Mac Heggety was found out in the desert country besides the buttes. Now I reckon to talk to yore brother, Miss Stella.'

'He's – he's – not here!' gasped the girl and she tried to slam the door in the sheriff's face.

The man was an old hand at this sort of treatment, and his boot was in the doorway, practically at the same time that Stella Camden slammed the door. She struggled to keep the sheriff out, but, with one hefty push, the indignant lawman rammed the door back.

'Thet ain't the right way to treat Bill Hapner!' he barked. 'Now where's thet young idjut! I want to parley with him.'

Wade Tulane heard the rapid tattoo of hooves from the alley behind the store and guessed the rest.

He smiled faintly. Seemed like Tommy Camden was getting out. But that kind of thing only pointed guilt at him. The young fool!

Sheriff Bill Hapner swung back from the store doorway and leaped down the boardwalk in order to get a better view of the departing horseman. There was only a momentary view of a dark shape on a galloping horse and the sound of hooves on the sun-baked road and then the rider flung the animal around a corner and was gone.

Wade noticed that the sheriff had drawn his gun, but he had not even cocked the hammer. Maybe the action of drawing was instinctive with the lawman. But it seemed he had not intended to shoot.

Bill Hapner swung his burly frame around and glared at the girl in the doorway.

'Crazy young galoot! I reckon he kilt Mac Heggety!'

'It was a fair fight!' cried the girl. 'And Mac Heggety and his brother, Rip, killed my father! We know they did! We —'

'Tommy can't take the law into his own hands!' snapped the sheriff. 'An' it won't do him any good to light out o' town.'

'You just scared him,' returned the girl. 'He won't take to the trails. He'll come back.'

'Where's he likely to go?' barked the sheriff.

'I – I – wouldn't know!'

'Shore gettin' to be a mighty lawless town!' grumbled Bill Hapner, and then he glanced at Wade Tulane. 'What the heck yuh doin' skulking there?'

Wade walked forward. 'Reckon I was about to call on Miss Camden when yuh moseyed up.'

'Who the hell are yuh?'

'Wade Tulane, Sheriff. A stranger in town,' and Wade watched the other's reaction narrowly.

The name seemed to mean nothing to Sheriff Bill Hapner. He stepped down from the boardwalk. 'I'm aiming to look for Tommy,' he warned. 'An' I want to hear the truth about Mac Heggety. An' take my advice, Miss Stella, don't go around sayin' Mac and Rip kilt yore father iffen yuh can't prove it. Mac is shore dead but Rip Heggety is plumb alive an' a pretty mean *hombre* at the best o' times.'

And with that the sheriff tramped away, bent upon his business.

Wade Tulane pursed his lips and turned to the girl. 'Shore seems like Tommy is in trouble. Wal, if it ain't any of my business jest say so, ma'am.' Lamplight gleamed on her pretty face and revealed her anxiety.

'You, again, Mr Tulane! Oh, I've heard all about you – how you helped Dave Latimer in that fight.'

'Jest did what the others would ha' done iffen they'd got around to it.'

'I hate Leo Sand!' She nearly stamped her foot.

34

Then she looked confused. 'Nothing would ever make me marry him! I know you've heard about that from Dave Latimer – he came along to have a talk with Tommy.'

Wade Tulane moved close to the girl, but half-turned so that he could scan the street. A rider came past. It was probably a cowboy riding in for entertainment. But Wade Tulane was a *hombre* with an inbred wariness, and he felt safe with his back to a wall.

'I'd like to help yuh, Miss Stella,' he muttered. 'I ain't nothin' but a wanderer an' yuh can tell me to shooshay if yuh figger it ain't none of my bizness. But killin' is a serious thing anywhere, even in a boom-town like this, an' Tommy will have a posse after him pretty soon iffen he don't come back an' explain.'

To his surprise, the girl said quickly: 'Have you got a horse ready?'

'Could fork the critter.' Wade nodded. 'Why, ma'am?'

'Get your horse, Mister Tulane, and come back here. I'll be changed from this dress into something suitable for riding. Perhaps you can help me find Tommy – now, tonight! I have a feeling I know where he'll be. Will you help me? You said you would?'

Wade felt inward surprise at his own words as he said: 'Shore do anythin' yuh want. Me – I'm a *hombre* with an idle loop. I'll go git my hoss.'

He strode away and heard the door shut behind him. He walked along, passing the Bonanza Hotel and the La Belle saloon, and came to the livery where he had left his horse.

He ascertained that the hostler was still with the animals in his care and curtly told the oldster to rub down the black horse. Wade went to his hotel. He went into his room and carried out his saddle gear. He left his rifle in the room although the saddle had a scabbard. He walked through the bar-room on his way out to the street.

He was not thinking about Leo Sand and he did not see the gambler eye him narrowly as he carried the saddle gear to the batwings and passed out into the street.

Wade saddled up in the livery and noted that the cayuse was fairly fresh after the few hours of rest. A short ride would do the animal no harm.

He led the horse out of the livery and paid the wrangler for the few hours of attention the animal had received, and then swung into the saddle. He jigged the horse up the street and then dismounted beside the drapery store.

Stella Camden was evidently an unusual girl for she had changed in the few minutes that had elapsed since he had left her. There was the sound of a horse's hooves from the alley at the side of the clap-board store and the girl rode out of the gloom on a pinto. Wade grinned, a shaft of light from the saloon across the way falling on his face and giving him that suddenly boyish look.

'Which way do we go?' he drawled.

She pointed down the street, to the east of the town. 'We'll ride that way. I think we'll find Tommy. I've been thinking it over and the sheriff is right. He must try to explain that it was a fair fight.'

Wade Tulane swung back to saddle leather. They jogged down the street, stirrup to stirrup. She had changed into blue jeans which were tucked into riding boots. She wore a buckskin jacket of evidently Indian handiwork. A small blue hat almost hid her fair hair, but a bit hung down over her ears. This much Wade saw in the light of a lantern they passed at a street corner and then they were in the shade again.

For some moments they rode on in silence. It was enough that he had volunteered to help her. She could explain something about the set-up in her own good time.

It was only a matter of minutes and they were heading out of Laredo, leaving the straggle of cabins and the stockyards that marked the outskirts of the town. The only light on the well-rutted trail leading east out of town came from a pale moon high among the merest wisps of clouds.

'Mac Heggety and Rip Heggety killed my father,'

she said suddenly in a low voice. 'But we've never been able to prove it. Perhaps I should tell you everything, Mister Tulane. I feel that I can confide in you.'

'Shore like to hear yuh say thet,' drawled Wade. 'Yuh can start by callin' me by my first name. Never could git used to anybody callin' me mister!'

The girl laughed slightly. 'All right. And, frankly sometimes the conventions bore me. So please call me Stella.'

Wade leaned on the saddle horn. 'It's a mighty bad thing thet yore father was killed, Miss Stella. Dave Latimer told me a bit about him. Now if yuh'll excuse a straight question – why should anyone want to kill yore father?'

'He was bushwhacked,' said the girl clearly. 'He never carried guns and he was shot down in the back – which makes it worse. As to your question, Wade, Tommy and I don't know yet why anyone would want to kill Daddy. He never harmed anyone. And I never knew that he had any enemies. That is until after he was dead. Then we began to suspect Mac Heggety and his younger brother, Rip. It's so hard to explain why we know they killed Daddy! But those two came to the store one day and offered to buy the place. We said we didn't want to sell. You'd have thought that rebuff would be sufficient, but practically every other day they returned and made offers that gradually became crazy.'

'What d'yuh mean by thet?' asked Wade.

'They offered more for the store than it is worth lock, stock and barrel!' cried the girl.

'Shore seems queer,' muttered Wade. 'But is thet all?'

'Oh, no! Tommy caught them one night rifling through the house at the back of the store. Tommy had taken me to a concert at the church hall and we'd returned perhaps a bit early because one of the performers did not turn up and the concert was quickly over.'

'Yeah?'

'Tommy and I went into the store from the front door – there is a door at the back which serves the house and there is an enclosed yard and stable. Tommy saw men moving in the living-room, and there was a light. Well, he dashed forward. He wasn't wearing a gun. He is actually too young to walk around like a gun-toting hard-case. He —'

The girl saw the rueful smile on Wade's face and, laughingly, she laid a hand on his arm, reaching across from her horse to do it.

'I didn't quite mean it that way! But I'm sure you'll agree that Tommy is still a boy and, anyway, Daddy had not encouraged him to handle guns. But he did, of course – like most young men around these parts he wanted to be a great shot and I know he practised secretly. Well, that is by the way. Tommy was not wearing a gun when he dashed into the living-room after those two men.'

'Two men, Stella?' queried Wade.

'Yes, two of them. But they were quick. They got out very fast and they had horses in the alley. They just raced away at full lope. We couldn't do anything to stop them. When we went back into the house we found it had been ransacked. Tommy and I thought it very strange that some money had not been taken. Then we found the lantern the two men had left. It had the initials "M.H." scratched on the side.'

'Mac Heggety?' questioned Wade.

'That's what we thought, and we told the sheriff. We went with him to the placer claim that the two Heggety brothers worked on the river. But they practically laughed in our face and denied the lantern belonged to them. Even the sheriff couldn't prove it. The initials happened to fit two other men – one in town and the other a placer miner. So we came away and had to forget the whole thing. But we knew who had killed Daddy. Mac Heggety and Rip! It was just one of those sure hunches – so hard to explain and yet founded on instinct.'

3

THE FIGHT

There was silence between Wade and the girl for a moment while they rode down the trail. Then he said: 'Hmm. From what yuh've said, it ain't likely that yore father was bushwhacked for nothin'. By thet, I mean the bustin' into yore house an' ransackin' means there is some kind of loco reasin for the actions of these two jaspers.'

'Only one now – Rip Heggety,' Stella reminded him, and he thought he detected some satisfaction in her voice.

He chuckled. 'Yep. One has hit the dust! Sure hope Tommy can prove it was a fair fight. Guess we'll have to find him. Where'd yuh figure he's gone? I reckon yuh're ridin' this trail for some reason.'

'Yes, I have an idea where he's gone,' said the girl, and she urged her horse into a canter. 'And that's why I've asked you to help. You pack guns and we might need them. I feel sure Tommy has headed for the River Shasta – to get hold of Rip Heggety and make him confess. He was hinting that when Sheriff Hapner knocked.'

'Thet ain't such a healthy idee for a young feller,' said Wade. 'I've got the notion thet Rip Heggety is a bit of a hellion.'

'He is – rough and wild! Let's ride faster.'

He touched spur rowels to his horse and the animal went into a full lope. The few hours' rest had done the creature some good. He did not know the trail, however, so he let the girl lead the way. Her pinto was a sure-footed cayuse.

The more Wade Tulane thought about it, the more he realized that Tommy Camden had a good move if he was bent on getting Rip Heggety to confess to the murder of his father. That would clear him of any charge of killing Mac Heggety without due cause. It was a good move, providing Rip would confess!

The trail twisted around some big buttes and then led through a plain dotted with scrub trees and cactus. The moonlight threw a wan illumination over the terrain. After a mile of this, Wade saw the land freshen with grass as well as the greedy cholla. Then they entered a gully which led right down to the side of a fair sized stream. This was the River Shasta, he knew without being told. He had never seen it before, but this was it.

As they rode along under the moon, the girl still leading the way, he speculated on the string of events that had gotten him into helping this girl. It wasn't a very strong chain and he could back out easily – but he didn't want to do that, not on any account! He could not analyse it. He was not a man without cares; he had the ever-present fear of being identified as a wanted man. He should have been minding his own business, but right now he was riding into a queer tangle.

All at once the ride brought them to the first of the placer miner camps. It was a familiar scene to Wade Tulane. It brought back memories of Jack Rawkin and the camp they had had in Colorado. A tighter expression settled over his face.

Lights glowed from inside tents, and fires studded the river bank. He heard the sound of strong-voiced men cursing, arguing and laughing. Horses whinnied somewhere near a clump of trees. Someone was hammering away, metal on metal. As they rode along the trail, he wondered if it was not time he took the lead. This was a place where trouble could whip up pretty fast. And where was Tommy Camden?

Wade rode abreast of the girl's pinto. 'Yuh know where this hellion, Rip Heggety, has his claim?'

'Yes, of course. It's at the end of this camp, by a big growth of willows.'

She pointed through the pale light. He nodded.

'Reckon I'll go first, Stella. What is it yuh want – jest git Tommy back to town out o' trouble?'

'I suppose so, unless he has made Rip Heggety talk in which case I'd love to haul that rough devil to the sheriff!'

'Guess thet's a tough assignment for a young feller. More likely he'll run into trouble.'

It seemed a startlingly prophetic remark, for as they jigged up to the clump of willows a din of bawling voices broke out. There was the slither of boots on shale and then gasps as men exchanged blows.

It was enough for Wade Tulane. 'Wait here!' he snapped at the girl, but he did not pause to see if she obeyed. He urged his mount forward; went down the slight incline to the edge of the river in a rapid rata-pan of hooves on gravel and stones.

At the end of the ride, he slid from his horse and strode towards two men who fought savagely as they pounded blow after blow at each other in the rigid upright stance of the times.

Wade saw Tommy Camden get the worst of the encounter in the five seconds that he hesitated as he wondered if he should let them fight it out. It was no wonder that the young fellow fell back. The other man, who was presumably Rip Heggety, had slammed a wicked punch into Tommy's guts. Granted this was a deadly brawl, it was still a terrible

44

punch. Tommy Camden staggered to the ground. The other rushed up and then crouched.

Wade knew what was coming. He'd seen that roughhouse trick many times. Rip Heggety figured to jump down on his opponent's body – maybe his face – with all the force of a miner's steel-studded boots!

Wade Tulane shot in, head down like a battering ram, just as Rip Heggety leaped.

The two collided, but not over the body of Tommy Camden for he had sensed what was coming and had rolled.

Wade Tulane's hatted head rammed into Rip Heggety's belly and stopped the man in mid-air, so to speak! Actually, he rammed back and fell to the earth, back thudding into the gravel and shale. Wade's hat fell off. He ignored it; advanced to the prone man.

Stella had not been wrong when she had hinted that Rip Heggety was rough and tough, a red-blooded young hellion. In spite of the severe impact, he scrambled up to meet Wade. His boots dug at the earth. One moment he was a bundle and then the next he was on his feet, hissing with fury. Wade got a glimpse of a contorted face that might at any other time been considered handsome in a reckless way. The hellion was dressed in dirty checked shirt and pants tucked into heavy boots. Obviously, he was no dandy of the town.

'I'll smash yuh, stranger!' he bawled. 'Then I'll beat this pup to a hash so thet he won't hell around killin' other men!'

Wade had time to reflect that Rip Heggety knew about his brother's death. He wondered how long he'd known. Not long, he figured. Sheriff Hapner had just started on an investigation so that meant the body had just been brought in.

His flash of thought terminated as the other *hombre* slammed out a fist that had the force of a swinging shovel. Wade hardly knew how he dodged it, but he did. Grimly, he realized he would have to bring all his powers to a peak if he wanted to whip this hellion. The momentum brought Rip Heggety close to him. Wade saw the savage expression uncomfortably close. He slammed his first punch – a right-handed swing that crashed on the other's face. At least he had scored!

It was the first of a series of relentless blows by both men. First, Wade had the advantage and then Rip Heggety had his man staggering back. Boots slithered raspingly all the time. Hoarse gasps were belted out of the men each time a blow slammed home. Wade fought grimly, coldly, realizing this man was no soft-liver. He had slammed punches in a style that would have been approved in a roped ring, but continuing this did not seem to appeal to Rip Heggety.

46

He suddenly charged in again and grappled with Wade. He swung Wade off his feet under the unexpected fury of the charge. The men crashed to the earth.

If Rip Heggety expected to get the upperhand out of the fall, he was disappointed, for Wade rolled savagely the moments his back rasped into the shale and gravel. He jerked the other man around and grabbed at his hands, seeking to stop the huge paws that sought his neck.

Wade rammed a fist into Rip Heggety's face and felt blood spurt. The other writhed like a roped steer. It seemed impossible to keep this savage man down, but Wade managed it. He slammed another fist into the face while the other wasted his chances in trying to throw Wade off his body. The blow dazed Heggety. Wade grabbed him by the hair and by his shirt and lifted the hellion up about a foot. Then he crashed him down again, the man's head ramming sickeningly against some rock. If the blow had momentarily dazed Rip Heggety, this other treatment kept him semi-concious. Wade Tulane repeated the grim process. He knew it was necessary with a roughneck like this. He twice crashed the *hombre*'s head against the ground. He felt the other's hands slacken and fall uncertainly. Rip Heggety was out of this world.

Wade got up, crouched over the man. Sure enough, the brute strength of Rip Heggety returned;

his mind cleared and rage threw him back into the battle.

But Wade Tulane had the upperhand. As he saw the other endeavour to rise, he slammed a wicked punch to the character's chin. Rip Heggety slumped again.

But he even tried it once more. He rolled suddenly after he had lain still for some long moments with Wade crouched over him. Rip Heggety's feet lashed out and then, following it up, he tried to rise.

Wade jumped to avoid the threshing boots and rammed the terrible blows once more to the other's head. Rip Heggety fell back. Wade straightened; shoved his hand to his gun and glared around.

There were onlookers in the darkness; men beside a tent; another, thumbs hooked in belt, staring and standing beside a camp fire; and yet another holding a horse. They showed no sign of going for a gun.

Rip Heggety stirred again and sat up. He did not try to start the fight again, but in accepting the beating, he glared at the man who had licked him. He did not go for his gun, evidently deciding there would be a better time and a better place. He was in no condition to attempt a fast draw.

Wade Tulane backed towards his horse. He sensed that Tommy Camden was further up the slope. It seemed the best thing to achieve was to get the young fellow back to Laredo.

He stopped and picked up his hat as it tangled with his feet.

Rip Heggety stood up and swayed. He braced his shoulders and wiped blood from his face.

'I'll remember yuh, stranger!' he snarled.

It was the second time an enraged *hombre* had said that to Wade Tulane since he had entered Laredo. There was nothing funny in a man adding to his enemies and Wade felt pretty grim as he backed to his horse. He sensed that Tommy Camden and his sister were further up the slope. Probably Tommy had collected his horse.

All at once Wade heard the rapid thud-thud of hooves on the trail. He wheeled and was in time to see Tommy Camden urging his horse into full lope.

Someone shouted: 'The sheriff!'

It was, indeed. And with the sheriff was another man, most probably a deputy. They thundered down the trail and only slowed their horses momentarily; then, the next instant, they were off in pursuit of Tommy Camden.

Wade Tulane cursed under his breath. This young fool was only making matters worse by taking to flight. Wade jumped to his horse and jigged it up the slope until he hit the trail, and there he was joined by Stella Camden. She stared fearfully at the vanishing, riders.

'The sheriff is after him! What shall we do?'

'Let's go ride the same way,' jerked Wade. 'If Hapner catches the young idjut, we want to be on hand to offer some parley.'

He lightly touched his horse with the rowels and the animal sprang into a full lope. Stella did the same. It was just as well they moved so suddenly, for a gun barked from the direction of Rip Heggety's camp. The slug whistled harmlessly through the night air, however, for Wade and the girl were already in motion.

They thundered away from the placer camp, following the river-bank trail. Camp fires spaced the river bank at almost regular intervals, and the dim shapes of miners could be seen either idling or engaged in some work. Little notice was taken of their swift ride. Reckless riders often came along the trail, and placer miners were the type who minded their own businesses. After riding nearly a mile along the rough trail and negotiating a narrow plank bridge over a steep gully, they encountered two riders astride blowing horses. It was the sheriff and his deputy and they seemed plenty mad.

Sheriff Bill Hapner recognized Stella in the gloom 'He got away!' he shouted. 'This trail forks and, by heck, we went down the wrong one for a few hundred yards afore I figured he'd taken the other trail!'

'We'll find him again, Sheriff!' cried the girl. 'And we'll clear up everything. Tommy only came down to this camp to make Rip Heggety confess that he and his brother killed my father. If Mac Heggety killed Daddy, that fact would clear Tommy, wouldn't it?'

'Still toting thet durned yarn!' barked Bill Hapner. 'How many times have I got to tell yuh I want proof! Mac and Rip Heggety had alibis the day yore Paw was killed.'

'Their ruffian pals would say anything for half a bottle of red-eye!' said the girl scornfully.

'Mebbe, but I can't git any proof thet them two hellions killed yore father – only wish I could, Miss Stella. An' now yore idjut brother goes and salivates Mac Heggety out in the desert.'

'It was a fair fight. They both drew guns. Tommy was nicked, but I'm glad it's not so bad as it looks.'

'Mebbe it was a fair fight – but it looks like yore brother ain't stayin' to explain. The goshdarned fool! He's just makin' things worse by runnin' away.'

'He – he's young and – and – inexperienced, Sheriff. He wasn't brought up to mix with gun-toters. And he's scared a bit, I think.'

'Yep, by heck he ought to be! I'd like to hear him explain how come he jest happened to be near Mac Heggety out in the desert beside the buttes. Seems mighty like he was trailin' Mac Heggety. How do I know it was a fair fight? Maybe Tommy jumped the other *hombre* an' got thet slug in his shoulder for fair exchange.'

'Mebbe yuh could give the younker the benefit o' the doubt,' put in Wade smoothly.

'Not if I can prove it murder!' barked the sheriff. 'I'm not handin' favours to any gink in this town. It's gettin' to be mighty lawless without me encouragin' men to go kill each other!'

Wade Tulane smiled thinly, the gloom and his Stetson hiding the flitting expression. He had a sudden hunch that Sheriff Bill Hapner's bark was worse than his bite. But he did not doubt the lawman was a stickler for duty and justice.

'Guess yuh know Miss Stella and Tommy caught two *hombres* ransacking their house jest after Mr Camden was killed and they figured them for the Heggety brothers,' he said casually.

'Yep, I know thet, but nobody caught those galoots at it. How d'yuh reckon I can pin things on men without some proof? Say – yuh horning into this bizness?'

'Mebbe. Yuh could say I'm givin' a hand.'

'Stranger, ain't yuh?' grunted the sheriff. 'Wade Tulane, huh! I remember the monicker.'

Wade rolled a tongue around inside his mouth and wondered if the name was going to strike the sheriff as something significant. Maybe he should have adopted another name when he had hit Laredo. Even so, he had met up with someone from the past. It might have been hard explaining to Ezra Sloan why he had taken a new name.

'Don't yuh figure there was somethin' mighty queer in two men ransacking William Camden's house so soon after his death?' pursued Wade.

Sheriff Hapner fingered his bristly moustache. 'Yep, it was mighty queer, I'll allow. If yuh can explain it, *hombre*, I'll shore be glad to listen.'

Wade leaned on the saddle horn. 'I don't know the answer any more than yuh do, but mebbe I'll find out. To my mind, Tommy and Miss Stella ain't had the right sort of galoot to help 'em discover what's goin' on. Shore seems queer thet Mac and Rip Heggety offered to buy the drapery store for more than it's worth. Then two jaspers – two mark yuh – ransack the house. What the blazes were they lookin' for?'

'I don't know, Tulane,' snapped Sheriff Hapner. 'Let me tell yuh somethin' – I got a mighty lawless town to deal with with killings an' robberies most every goshdarned day. I jest can't look hard at everythin'. I bin talkin' to the mayor about more deputies, but he hums an' haws about the dunned cost and says the taxes won't stand for it. Goldarn it, I don't know why I don't buy me a ranch an' mind my own business! If I had the dinero, I reckon I'd do thet mighty fast!'

Wade smiled as he watched the highly incensed sheriff. Then the lawman turned his horse.

'We're hittin' the trail back to town! Yuh can save

me a lot o' trouble by bringin' thet idjut brother o' yourn in for questioning. In any case, he'd be safer in the hoosegow because Rip Heggety is goin' to be meaner than a mountain cat. It was jest about twenty minutes ago thet a prospector brought Mac Heggety's body in and I reckon Rip ain't known about it long enough to go hellin' for his guns. Aw, gosh, why do I have to be a John Law!'

With this disgusted remark, Sheriff Hapner spurred his horse forward. His silent deputy followed him down the trail.

Wade jigged his black horse close to the girl's pinto. 'The sheriff is about right,' he said grimly. 'Rip Heggety will be plenty mad. He's a rough jasper. Tommy is in a bad spot.'

Stella stared around the gloomy terrain with a touch of desperation. 'We've got to find Tommy! We've got to prove to the sheriff it was a fair fight. Then we've got to protect Tommy until Rip Heggety cools down.'

'Yep.' Wade pushed his horse forward. 'Let's git goin'. We're too near the placer camp to be healthy. I guess yore Tommy is a little impulsive, huh? He should ha' known he hadn't a coyote's chance of makin' a ranny like Rip Heggety confess to anything. Why, thet feller is mighty tough! An' Tommy has a wounded shoulder. Yep, a headstrong young cuss if nothin' else!'

They rode along the trail, taking the fork that the sheriff had not explored. There was a slight chance they might encounter Tommy Camden. He might have halted or hidden.

'I've just about dragged you into troubles,' said Stella suddenly, with a little laugh. 'And, frankly, there isn't any real reason why you should get in bad with men like Rip Heggety for our sakes. I wouldn't blame you if you decided to stop helping us.'

Wade Tulane smiled his faint smile. It was a strange mixture of the secretive and the shy, and the twist changed those firm lips.

'Yuh got the wrong idee, Miss Stella,' he drawled. 'I'm a *hombre* on the loose. I ain't handy with words – but I wouldn't back down from helpin' yuh if there were ten jaspers like Rip Heggety plaguin' yuh!'

Even as he uttered this lame statement, he knew it was not the actual truth. He had a definite urge to help this slender, fair-haired girl because he had an insistent desire to know her better!

They rode down the trail and he noticed they had veered away from the river bank. There was no sign out here of men's activities. Only the moon made any illumination. Great cacti that grew upwards with big trunks took on the appearance of weary old men in the pale moonlight. There were clumps of mesquite and catclaws looking like pleasant green bushes and not the thorny things they actually were.

55

Moonlight on the desert is a mystical experience for most people and there was a curious feeling of unreality about the ride through the arid land. Wade had to remind himself that they were seeking a young fellow who was, at the moment, hiding from the law and sought by a ruffian wanting revenge.

They trotted on as fast as the track would allow. There was no chance of looking for sign in this light. Wade felt they were probably on a wild-goose chase.

And then, as they rounded a hulking rocky sentinel, a voice called to them:

'Sis! I'm here!'

4

'SAY YORE PRAYERS'

When he realized that Stella and Wade Tulane were not attended by the sheriff and his deputy, Tommy rode out to meet them. He jogged his brown mare from out of the cover of the huge rock. Another moment and they made a little group.

'You sure helped me out o' that mess, Tulane,' said the young fellow frankly. 'Dave Latimer told me about yuh, too. That was when he called to ask how come I'd got a wound. Maybe I'm a fool, Tulane. I couldn't have beaten Rip Heggety with my shoulder the way it is.'

'Yore best plan is to git back to town,' began Wade.

'An' have Bill Hapner clap me in jail!' interrupted the other. 'Or mebbe Rip Heggety come gunnin' for me?'

'I got a hunch yuh can talk the sheriff into acceptin' yore account of the shooting-match between yuh an' Mac Heggety,' snapped Wade. 'He's the law around here.'

'That still leaves Rip. I couldn't even try draw guns with that jasper. I've heard he's fast.'

'I'll see yuh don't have to draw against Rip,' said Wade.

'You mean that?' gulped the youngster. 'Gosh, I admit I'm scared. I – I – I'm not cut out for this work! Maybe you don't know, Wade Tulane, but I work on the *Laredo Journal.* I'm kind of reporter – just gather bits of news for old Ben Smith, my boss. It isn't the sort o' work that fits me for tackling *hombres* like Rip Heggety.'

'Yuh shore tackled his brother,' said Wale slowly. 'I'd like to hear yore account of thet gun-play. How come yuh killed the galoot, Tommy? Give me some straight answers. Why were yuh out in the desert the same time and same place? How'd yuh beat him on the draw?'

'I'll tell you, Tulane,' muttered the young lad. 'Just like I told Stella and Dave Latimer when he called. I rode into Mac Heggety by accident. I didn't trail him. An' you know where I first sighted him? He was riding mighty queerly through the canyon where father was found dead!'

'Yeah? How come yuh were there, too?'

'Just chance. I got the urge to ride through the canyon and as I had some free time, I saddled up and rode out. I never expected to see Mac Heggety there. I was just wandering around, I guess. I've always wondered why father was out of town the day he got that damn bushwhack bullet. He never travelled much. I wanted to ride through the canyon just to figure out some hunches why Dad was out there the day he died. And then I saw Mac Heggety. He was a good many years older than Rip and more cunning than rough. He was riding slowly an' stopping every few yards to examine the canyon wall. I watched him for some time and then my hoss neighed. He jerked like he'd been caught out – kinda queer, I thought. I wasn't backing out, and so I just sat my horse as he rode up.'

'That when the shootin' started?' hazarded Wade Tulane.

'Yep. He just rode towards me, across that canyon floor, an' then I knew he was going for his smoke-pole. Sure, he didn't draw, but I just guessed. He rode up. Then he went for the Colt. I was all tensed, Mister Tulane.' Tommy Camden's speech slurred. 'This was the first time I'd ever tried to match a draw with another *hombre*. I'd had practice with old cans but – but —'

'Yuh beat him anyway,' said Wade quietly.

'I – I – never knew how I did it! Mac Heggety had

been toting guns before I was born! He knew how to handle a smokepole all right. But I beat him. My slug took him right in the heart. I got his slug, too. In the shoulder.'

'Yuh probably beat him on account of nervous tension,' said Wade. 'Thet would speed up yore gunplay.'

'Maybe. Thanks for the explanation.' Tommy laughed raggedly. 'I just rode out o' that canyon in a scare. Don't ask me why! Just because I don't kill a man every day – that's all, I guess! Wasn't long after that I ran into you. I was still scared an' didn't want to be stopped. I guess I acted crazy.'

Wade slapped the other on his good arm. 'Say, tell the account to the sheriff an' I reckon he'll accept yore story. Shore it was a fair fight. It was him or yuh. Let's ride back to town afore Bill Hapner has yuh on a Wanted poster!'

There was a laugh at this. 'Sure hate to think I was a wanted man,' grinned Tommy. 'I've written paras about outlaws and always figured there was something to pity about a galoot who is being hunted.'

Wade stiffened and then nodded. For the first time in weeks he had forgotten that he was a wanted man. And now the youngster's laughing remark brought the realization that his time in Laredo could be very short. A Wanted poster might arrive with any mail left at the sheriff's office. He might have to ride

60

out, leave Stella and Tommy with their troubles still rankling. In fact, he might be lucky if he got the chance to ride out. 'Let's hit the trail!' he said harshly. 'Yore best plan is to talk to the sheriff, young feller. You'll be the biggest idjut alive if yuh figure to keep on the dodge.'

'I'll have to sharpen up my gun practice,' muttered Tommy, 'because Rip will be after me.'

'He's not yore class,' Wade almost snarled. 'Jest leave him to me!'

'That's mighty fine of you. I guess Stella an' me need friends. You think I should ride back an' go to Bill Hapner? He scared me when he called at the store.'

'I say you're goin' back,' said Wade grimly. 'No more parley! Let's git goin'.'

But Stella wanted to have her say!

'Wasn't it queer that Tommy should find Mac Heggety riding through the canyon as if he was looking for something?'

Wade smiled faintly. 'Seems plumb queer, I agree. The way I see it, there's one *hombre* who knows all the answers – Rip Heggety. He could tell yuh why Dad was kilt and why the store was searched – an' even why they want to buy the place. Thet last one is easy. They wanted to buy the store an' house to find something. When they couldn't buy it off yuh, they reckon to find what they wanted in a search. Wal, maybe we

61

ought to look around the store an' house ourselves. An' maybe I ought to ride out to thet canyon tomorrow.'

'I'll show you the place,' said Tommy eagerly. 'Unless Bill Hapner sticks me in the jail-house!'

They started on the ride back and, at Tommy's direction, took a bead across country so that they would not cross the path of the placer camps. They entered Laredo some time later. The saloons were about the only busy places and their light threw patches across the main stem as the party of three rode along. True all Laredo was not rowdy and bent on rough pleasure-seeking. There had been a meeting in the little adobe church that night. Some of the townsfolk found pleasure in gathering to hear a lecturer at the council chamber. The more solid ranchers had met in the Stockman Hotel to talk business and debate the shipment of cattle by the newly-opened railroad. And many of the neater homes in the town afforded scope for family gatherings. There was little thought of this in Wade Tulane's mind as they rode up to the sheriff's office and tied their horses to the hitch-rail. In the manner of the times, Wade gallantly helped Stella Camden to mount the few steps to the porch. One might have thought she was wearing a bustle instead of very boyish blue jeans, shirt and buckskin jacket.

On reaching the notice-board outside the office,

Wade slowed and gave it a wary glance. He saw the pictures of two wanted men. His own jib was not there. He stayed long enough to flick a glance at the descriptions of other outlaws of whom there was no photograph. The descriptions did not fit him and neither did the charges. Breathing easily once more, he waited. Tommy Camden had hammered on the closed door. There was a suggestion of a lamp behind the blind on the window, so maybe Sheriff Hapner was in the office. Like most of these places, the office also had living-quarters and a jail. The sheriff lived on his job.

Bolts were pulled and then Bill Hapner stood outlined in lamp-light in the doorway. He did not seem surprised to see his visitors.

'Thought you'd see some sense,' he commented, and he rubbed his bristly moustache. He swallowed something. It seemed that the sheriff had been taking in some food.

They went inside the office. Wade stared at the sheaf of papers on the desk beside the mug of coffee and the plate of sandwiches. More Wanted notices!

'I want to tell you what happened out by the desert buttes,' faltered Tommy Camden.

'Not before time!' barked the sheriff. 'Yuh could ha' saved me some trail-poundin'!'

Tommy launched out on the same story he had related to Wade Tulane, neither glossing over parts nor distorting the facts. It was just as well he did not, for Bill Hapner shot some shrewd questions at him that might have tripped him up had he not been telling the truth. The tale took some time in telling and as Bill Hapner doggedly ate his sandwiches and barked questions, Wade felt kind of hungry! He felt he needed his supper!

At last the sheriff gave his pronouncement. 'Yuh can go, young feller. I ain't lockin' yuh up. Guess it was a fair fight at that. Fer Gawd's sake, don't git into any more trouble! This town is shore goin' to perdition. I keep tellin' the mayor that, but all he does is hum an' haw!'

'He won't get into any more grief,' drawled Wade, 'but I ain't so shore others ain't fixin' to hand it his way. I mean the galoot Rip Heggety won't take yore judgment, Sheriff.'

'Git!' barked Bill Hapner. 'I can't protect every doggone man in this town! But I'll talk to Rip Heggety tomorrow. Ain't no more I can do.'

They went out to the horses at the hitching-rail. Wade was thinking: maybe now I can git some supper! Maybe Miss Stella can cook a pie and maybe she'll invite a friend to chow!

It was wishful-thinking and yet it came true. The girl did offer just that hospitality!

'Yeah, you come in and have a bite,' said Tommy eagerly. 'I don't know how to thank yuh, Mister Tulane.'

'Don't try, and call me Wade.'

The meal was a great success and the wanderer discovered that the girl was a grand cook, as indeed she had had to be ever since her father had been made a widower.

Although he prolonged the pleasant visit, Wade had to leave. His horse was still at the tie-rail outside and it would not do to neglect the animal so that it caught an ague. He would have to leave and take the horse to the livery.

'I'll see yuh tomorrow about thet ride to the canyon,' he said gravely.

'Shore, and if I'm tied to my work, maybe Sis can show you the place,' said Tommy innocently.

Wade nodded and took his leave.

The store door shut behind him with a jangle of the bell. He was about to step forward across the boardwalk to get his horse when an over-anxious voice snarled from across the street.

'I got a bead on yuh, feller. Say yore prayers!'

Wade froze. It was purely an involuntary action. His keen eyes searched the dark recesses on the other side of the street. The voice had snarled from some locked-up buildings. As the first two seconds of the grim position ticked off, Wade knew the man did not intend to shoot and get it over as quickly as possible. No, the hidden gunman wanted to play his victim as a cat does with a mouse.

Frantically, Wade tried to discern the slightest movement from the deep gloom across the way, but there was not even a variation of shade upon shade. The man was well and truly hidden. To go for hardware was to invite the death slug, for the hidden man evidently had his gun lined up.

With every nerve and muscle tensed, Wade Tulane stood on the boardwalk and felt cold things crawl up his spine. He knew Rip Heggety was across the street. Somewhere in the darkness the man stood and gloated.

'Yuh're a blastit interferin' skunk, mister,' came the cold voice again. 'Yuh know somethin' – I shore hate to have to kill yuh as easy as this! I'd sooner smash yuh to pulp bit by bit. I ain't fergettin' yuh beat me up down by the river. By Gawd, I reckon yuh were lucky. Yuh wouldn't do it again!'

'Throw down thet gun an' come out o' there and try me with yore fists,' Wade jerked. 'If yuh want it that way, don't play yourself out o' some satisfaction, *hombre*!'

A snarl greeted the suggestion. 'Go to hell! Yuh figger to talk yuh way out, don't ya? Start prayin', feller. Yuh crossed a hellion when yuh crossed me!'

'Yuh so yeller yuh got to hide!' taunted Wade quickly. 'Come on out an' give me a chance to draw!'

Desperately, he hoped for some reaction. Even if the other came forward and made it a straight gun-fight, he doubted if his hands would move fast enough. Right now he was stiff with over-tensed muscles.

'Nuthin' doin'!' chuckled the other. 'I'm jest salivating yuh, feller. I knew I'd git yuh comin' out o' that house. I saw yore hoss at the tie-rail. After yuh git yores, I'll fix thet young snakeroo, Tommy Camden! Dad-blame me if I don't! I'll fix him just as soon as I'm ready.'

Wade dived. Like lightning, he figured no man could spit out even a hundred words without relaxing a fraction.

He dived for the stone water-trough he had noted right from the start of the play. It stood at least ten yards away, at the edge of the boardwalk. Normally, he would have opined that no man could beat a slug and travel ten yards at the same time. But the impossible is always achieved by a man in a moment of terrific effort.

He shot for the cover of the stone horse-trough in a tremendous rush that ended in a dive so forceful that he thudded into the trough and shook it on its secure foundations. Simultaneously, Rip Heggety's gun barked twice. The slugs followed Wade in his desperate leap, just missing by inches owing to his terrific momentum. Then Wade was huddled behind the trough and his hands tugged at his two guns.

He gulped breath. Safe, so far! Grimly, he did not

underrate his adversary. Rip Heggety was in the hellion class, all right!

Wade Tulane poked out the hogleg in his right fist and slammed two shots into the darkness across the narrow street. He wanted to get some action now that he had cover. He wanted to shove Rip Heggety out of that deep gloom he had chosen for his hiding-place. He chanced a glance across the street as his shots plugged the darkness. Muzzle-flame spat viciously from a certain point and a slug bit into the earth only inches from Wade Tulane. He forced back the impulse to duck; he sighted on the spot where the orange flame had flashed. He triggered twice again and then rammed back into cover behind the horse-trough, his head well down.

To his disgust, there was no cry of pain in answer to his shots. So he had not hit the jasper!

Wade slammed two more shots over the top of the trough, just in case Rip Heggety had sighted on the corner of the object and was waiting for Wade to show his head.

The shots once again tore into the building across the street. Wade ducked, and then reloaded his sixshooter, slipping shells into it with grim speed.

He heard the sound of an approaching man behind him, from the corner of the alley down the side of the drapery emporium. A voice hissed:

'It's me, Tommy!'

'Keep back,' gritted Wade. 'It's Rip Heggety across the street!'

'I want to help you kill him!'

'Yuh keep out o' this, young feller!' snarled Wade. 'Thet jasper is skunky an' cunning as a coyote! Keep back!'

As if to emphasize this comment, a ratapan of shots bit all around the stone trough. Chips of rock dug at Wade and he had to shut his eyes tight. He waited.

All those shots meant the other man had emptied his guns. Three seconds after the last slug bit viciously into the trough, Wade Tulane launched out on another terrific dive – this time across the width of the street. He shot over so fast that showers of grit spurted from his boots. His left-hand gun blazed with every yard he covered. This was a form of cover, but he did not let this slow him. Speed was just as valuable as the Colts. He hit the side of the building opposite the drapery store and flattened while he dragged in a couple of deep breaths. He then reloaded, concious that this rumpus was certainly eating the shells. But he was on the same side of the road as Rip Heggety. Now to trick the man. Wade took off his hat and slid it gingerly around the corner of the building. He let his fingers slide to within an inch of the end of the clapboard wall and figured that was far enough.

All before his last thought ended, a shot cracked the night air and the hat whisked away. It fell to the dust some yards away.

Wade did not spend any time regretting the hole that would be in his hat. He slid back along the clapboard wall of the building and sidled around the rear of the place. He wanted to take Rip Heggety in the rear. Not that he underestimated the man. Already, Rip Heggety might realize Wade figured to circle him.

Wade was sidling along the back of the square building when he heard an enraged shout from somewhere down the street.

'Drop yore guns, yuh hellions, an' quit razing this town! This is the sheriff!'

Wade grinned thinly. Bill Hapner had come along to investigate the shooting. But words did not mean much to a hellion like Rip Heggety.

The next corner of the wood building was reached and Wade paused. Then he chanced the look he had to take. It was a quick darting movement of the head, no more. During that second he got a glance into the alley and figured it seemed empty. There was not that deep darkness that shrouded the front of the building.

He slid around into the alley, his guns the foremost thing of all. He got around the sharp corner, continued to sidle down the clapboard wall. His boots hunted into the dust silently with each step. Obviously Rip Heggety was still hidden in the shadows made by an overhanging porch at the front. Not by a solitary sound must he suspect Wade Tulane's whereabouts. Another angry shout bawled up the street.

'Git out o' thet, yuh ornery jaspers! I figger to have law an' order in this town! Hit the trail!'

Wade thinned a smile over his firm lips. Maybe the sheriff did not know who were engaged in the gunplay. Not that Sheriff Bill Hapner would care. All disturbers of the peace were poison to him apparently.

Reaching the next corner of the building Wade halted. This was the danger point. When he slid around this corner, it would have to be with guns ready to blaze inside a shattered second.

Not unnaturally, he paused to nerve himself. He was just a galoot and his courage could ebb or strengthen as circumstances dictated. Then in another grim second a sombre mood possessed him and gave him the impetus he needed. He was forming a hatred of Rip Heggety and that was enough.

He slid around the sharp corner, two guns poking a way through thin air.

5

LEO SAND'S OFFER

Wade saw the other man instantly.

Rip Heggety was in a doorway. That was why the shadows had enfolded him so completely. Looking down the side of the building, Wade could see the man's dark form as varying shade against the darkness that had served him so well.

Wade triggered, his guns needing no levelling. Even as he shot, everything was confusion. Actions were contained in a matter of seconds. He triggered, but Rip Heggety had sensed his presence at the last possible moment. His guns roared out and added to the din. Orange flame lanced the gloom under the overhanging porch.

Wade Tulane had thought to gain the advantage, but everything was based on such slender factors such as an unforseen split-second movement on someone's part.

He heard his guns roar, but he never had the chance to smell the gunsmoke.

With the crashing of guns, he felt an agonising, searing pain in his head. Blinding lights shot through his vision and then faded into darkness.

He did not know that he fell as the darkness rushed into his brain. In fact, Wade Tulane did not know anything as he thudded to the planked ground.

As to Rip Heggety, he had the luck of his kind. He jerked when he saw Wade on the corner and he fired frantically, backing into the deep doorway almost with one movement.

He knew it was time to get out. He had that impulse and he put into effect. He rammed against the locked door with all his hard, almost bull-like, strength. The door gave and he tumbled into the space beyond.

Moments later Rip Heggety wrenched open a door at the back of the building and he ran out into the night. His boots crunched violently and quickly into grit and dust as he made his getaway. He was going for his hidden horse.

He was not sure – but he thought Wade Tulane had been hit.

That was true. Wade did not hear the rapid thud of hooves as the hellion rode off. Wade never knew anything about the way people swiftly collected in the street. He didn't know that Stella Camden was among the first to reach him.

But he did open his eyes to stare at the girl, wonderingly and painfully at first. His head ached. It seemed simply a ball of shooting pains, and his eyes were heavier than lead. He made the clasical remark.

'Whar am I?'

'In Miss Stella's bedroom!' barked a voice. It was Sheriff Hapner. 'And yuh got a nifty crease down yore cranium, Mister Tulane. 'Nother half-inch and yuh would be a candidate for boot-hill!'

'Now don't bother him, Sheriff!' pleaded the girl. 'I wish the doc was here, but you say he's out at the B Bar M on a child-birth case.'

'He'll git over this,' grunted Bill Hapner, rising. 'He's in good hands, I reckon. And he's one o' these hardy *hombres* what can stand being thrown over a cliff by the looks o' things! Reckon he'll be wantin' the hide o' Rip Heggety soon as he can swing his feet off this bed!'

'That murderous swine!' grated Tommy Camden from the foot of the bed. He held some strips of cloth which he had torn into bandages. 'He laid an ambush for Wade – right outside our house! I don't know what happened exactly. First thing I knew was hearing those shots. I went out the back to see if I could help.'

'Good thing yuh had the savvy to use the back door an' not the front,' said Sheriff Hapner dryly.

Tommy swung to him angrily. 'What d'you figure to do about this, Bill Hapner?'

The sheriff's bristly moustache twitched as he barked: 'Nuthin'! I can't stop rannigans throwin' lead. I can't stop fair fights. I'd like to because it ain't law an' order. But the way this goshdarned town is goin' it's too much for one man and two deputies! I've told the mayor thet, but all he does is hum an' haw! If Tulane kills Heggety in fair fight, it ain't goin' to worry me none. But if either jasper commits a murder, I'll see him git a trial – and a hangnoose party!'

And with that warning, for what it was worth, the sheriff of Laredo stamped out of the room.

When Tommy and Stella glanced back at Wade Tulane, he had swung his legs down to the floor. He sat and fought back the swimming sensation. Stella turned to him with a little cry of concern. 'Oh, you can't move yet!'

'I got to git on my feet, Miss Stella,' he muttered. 'Shucks, I'm alive. So I didn't git Rip Heggety?'

'He got away. He had a horse somewhere.'

'Yeah, guess he would have. Wal, he didn't salivate me!' and Wade attempted a grin but it brought on shooting pains in his head and he grimaced.

'You really need Doc Thorne but he's out of town,' said Stella. 'The slug creased the side of your head. I've cleaned it and now you need a bandage.'

She was very firm about it and he had to submit to having the bandage wound around his head. But he wouldn't lie back after it. After his first few glances around the room, he knew it was the girl's bedroom by the feminine touches. Gay curtains and vases of flowers met his glance. A dress with tacking stiches lay on the edge of a sewing-machine. There was a faint perfume in the air. Wade felt vaguely embarrassed. He got off the bed and stood up – an effort, but he made it. He was conscious that his dusty clothes, heavy boots and thick shirt were strangely out of place in this girl's room. He had a feeling that, in spite of his ablutions in the hotel earlier that day, he still smelled of horses.

'Guess I'd better go,' he said, with his strangely shy grin. 'Mebbe I won't walk into grief this time, huh? See yuh tomorrow about thet ride to the canyon.'

His black horse had been tied to the rail all during the rumpus and, of course, had calmed since the shooting. He unhitched it and swung slowly to the saddle. He turned the horse and rode back to the livery. He left the animal to the old hostler and did not bother even to loosen the cinch. The wrangler could do that. Wade walked wearily into the Bonanza Hotel and made his way up to his room. A few men still leaned against the bar counter, but Wade never bothered to look them over.

In his room, he locked the door and lit the lamp.

He went to the window and saw it was a sheer drop to the yard below, so he left the window half-open. Although the night brought comparative coolness in these parts, the air was still warm and sluggish in the room.

He knew the slug crease had stopped any thought he might have of riding after Rip Heggety. He felt weary. Any further tangle with that rannigan would have to wait.

He dropped off his boots. He took off his belts and hung them on the brass rail at the head of the bed. He felt the bandage around his cranium and thought the bleeding had stopped. He considered undressing and then, with a grunt decided against. He flipped back the top blanket and lay on the bed, pulling the covering back over his body. As his head sank to the pillow, he went to sleep. He would lie like that until sun-up or something interrupted his rest.

It was as well for Wade Tulane's peace of mind that he did not see Leo Sand ride out of Laredo some time later, when the news of the shooting had spread over the saloons. Leo Sand took the trail down to the River Shasta, and the determined way he rode his pony showed he had made up his mind about a certain course of action.

He rode into the placer camp and stopped to ask a question of a man at the nearest tent.

'Rip Heggety? Yep. He's got a claim down by them

willows – turn o' the river – mebbe yuh kin see 'em?'

Leo Sand nodded and rode on, satisfied with the hint. He was not sure he would find the man he wanted immediately. He was prepared to wait a bit, anyway. He knew that Rip Heggety had tried to kill Wade Tulane, the stranger to Laredo. He knew the salient facts. It had gone around the saloon how Tulane had beat up Heggety down by the river and that the redblooded miner had sought revenge with guns.

Leo Sand had seen Wade return to the Bonanza Hotel, his head bandaged. It seemed that the interfering swine had the devil's own luck!

When Leo Sand finally located the placer claim by the willows, he did, in fact, find Rip Heggety there. The sullen young miner rose from the camp-fire and stood with one hand on a gun-butt, his feet planted apart.

'What the heck d'yuh want?'

'You know me?'

'Yeah – Sand, the gambler. I've seen yuh in the saloons.'

Leo Sand dismounted and carelessly flung his pony's reins over a soft willow branch. He came forward, his white face smiling flatly. 'I want a talk with yuh, *amigo.* Just heard how yuh tangled with Wade Tulane, thet damned stranger who's just rode in. Yuh know he's still alive?'

The angry look still decorated Rip Heggety's lean face. 'Yep. I heerd. What's it to yuh?'

'I wish you'd killed the swine,' said Leo Sand, and he brought out a package of the new-type factory-made cigarettes and offered them to the other man.

Rip Heggety took the smoke, examined it curiously and then picked up a reddened bit of wood from the fire. Both men lit up.

'So do I wish the jasper was dead,' he grunted. 'An' iffen he crosses my trail again, he will be dead. I don't stand for any jasper beatin' me up.' He glared at the black-suited gambler. 'He bashed my goddam head against the rock! Why, I've a good mind to ride back an' blast him where I find him!'

'He's in bed,' sneered Leo Sand. 'Maybe he ain't so hardy – I dunno.'

'What's yore complaint?' snapped Rip Heggety.

'He crossed me. I was in a fight with a gink called Latimer, an' Tulane shot a gun out of my hand. Near blamed took my hand away! Me – a gambler – my hand —'

'Ornery cuss, ain't he?' sneered Rip Heggety. He dragged on the cigarette and nearly consumed half of it. 'He just hits the burg an' starts raisin' hell all round. But I'll git him. I'll git him jest when I'm right and ready! I'll even with thet young catamount, Tommy Camden, too. I'll teach him to throw lead at my brother! That young cuss killed Mac!'

'I know about that. The news got around. And it looks like the sheriff lapped up that young feller's yarn because Tommy Camden is back home – he ain't in the hoosegow.'

Rip Heggety said venomously: 'I'm addin' him to my list, but I got somethin' to settle with the young cuss first. Before he heads for Boot-hill there's somethin' I want.'

'Yuh could clean up all around, a galoot like you,' said Leo Sand smoothly. 'Fix Tulane an' Tommy Camden. I don't know what it is yuh want off the younker, but I want the girl – Stella!'

'Hell – wimmen!' sneered the other. 'That yore angle?'

'Shore. I don't give a dumn what yuh think, I want Stella Camden. I wanted to marry her – she damned well turned me down, yessir!' Leo Sand's white face was suddenly taut with anger and sullen pride. 'Turn me down! Yuh git her damned brother out o' the way – and thet Tulane *hombre* – and I'll be mighty glad.'

'That all?' jeered Rip Heggety. 'Guess yuh want me to do yore dirty work!'

'I'll pay you!'

'Hell! I got a placer here thet pays off when I spend some time workin' it. And I got idees for more dinero – big money! Yeah, real big money, mister. I don't want yore damned silver dollars. Gold is more my line.'

'I'll help you git Tulane – and Tommy Camden for that matter!' snapped Leo Sand. 'Yuh want a hand – or a tipoff – count on me.'

'Yuh're not bein' so smart. I'll git those two buzzards in any case without yore help.'

'I just want to make sure,' began the gambler. 'Just wanted to let yuh know you can count on me.'

Rip Heggety turned sullenly to the fire and kicked the embers. 'I got pals already. Hey, Dutch, come on out o' thet tent. We got company.'

Rip had to go to the tent and shake a man inside. Then when he returned, there was a big bearded miner with him, a man who seemed to be plastered with river mud. His trousers and shirt were caked with it and it was in his beard. He had a leathery, round face and narrow, glinting eyes.

'Here's a feller who knows how to stack the cards, Dutch. So don't play him or mebbe he'll take thet damned cache away from yuh!' And Rip Heggety laughed recklessly as he made the crude introduction.

'Don' wan' to gamble witt anyones right now,' mumbled Dutch. His accent slowed his speech. 'Iss keepin' gold. Dere will be time when Dutch big rich mans.'

'My pard,' sneered Rip Heggety. 'He works like hell. He'll fight any time I ask. Don't know that I need yore help, Mister Sand.'

'You might,' snapped the other. 'All right, I've said my piece. You know how I feel. Jest one thing – is it right you and Mac killed William Camden those few weeks back?'

Rip Heggety laughed harshly.

'Yuh git plumb to hell, Mister Sand! I ain't sayin' no and I ain't sayin' yes.' And his laughter increased to a bellow as if he considered there was something very funny in all this.

Leo Sand turned to his pony. 'I don't give a damn. Soon as that girl is alone, she'll be right glad to have me around. Remember that, Heggety – that's what I want.'

The air was full of laughter as Dutch joined his partner in the coarse merriment. Dutch had a voice fit to waken the dead spirits in the distant City of Ghosts, an old labyrinth of caves and homes carved out of solid rock by an age-old tribe of Indians and now a haunt for coyotes outside Laredo.

Leo Sand had to ride away. The interview had been a bit of a failure. And he had shown Rip Heggety that he sided with him. That might be important if anything tricky cropped up. He rode his pony away from the camp, conscious that he had said his piece. And he meant everything he had said about Stella Camden. By thunder, he did!

He did not doubt that Rip Heggety and Mac had killed William Camden although the reason for this seemed shrouded in mystery. Now Mac Heggety was dead. Rip would surely get Tommy Camden for that act. And he would get Wade Tulane. Maybe Rip Heggety would act that night. But if he went into Laredo he might encounter the sheriff or a deputy. Maybe Rip Heggety would want to fight it out in gunsmoke, spurning cold-blooded murder. These tough hellions had that much pride in their guns.

Leo Sand sneered inwardly at the stupidity of these ideas. He urged his pony on. There was maybe time for a few hands of cards in one of the saloons before the customers began to hit the hay.

6

BURNING BULLETS

Wade Tulane felt a lot better the next morning as he examined the slug crease on the side of his head. The hot bullet had taken skin and hair away and it might leave a scar. He smiled faintly into the mirror as he considered that was better than a one-way trip to Boothill!

He considered the whole set up: Rip Heggety wanted him dead. And Rip Heggety would get Tommy Camden on the end of a Colt as vengeance for the death of his brother. But there was something else; something behind the killing of William Camden, draper. Why should the Heggety brothers kill a draper? Why should they try to buy the shop?

With these thoughts in mind, Wade remembered he had practically promised to ride out to the canyon where William Camden had been found dead.

He breakfasted at the Bonanza Hotel. Then he

went out and called at Stella's drapery store. He was the first customer that morning. He grinned as the girl came smilingly to greet him.

'Come into the living-room,' she began, but he held up a hand.

'I want to buy a hat,' he said solemnly. 'I lost mine last night – an' anyway I guess it has a hole in it.'

'We have some Stetsons – sombreros —' stammered the girl. 'And —'

He stared across the counter at the pile of thick, hardwearing shirts favoured by range riders. 'Maybe I ought to buy me a new shirt! Yep, an' I guess a galoot can always do with socks.'

The girl brought out three Stetsons which were telescoped into each other. Sorting them out, she placed them on the counter. 'I think you'd better try one, Wade!' And she laughed. 'Are you trying to drum up trade for me?'

'Nope. I really need a new hat an' a shirt an' a pair o' socks.' He tried on a fawn Stetson and glared critically across at a mirror. 'Got a nice brim. Guess this one will keep the sun out o' my eyes.' He paused. 'Tommy away at his job?'

'Yes. He had to go.'

'Howsabout thet ride out to the canyon? Don't rightly know why I want to see the place but Tommy's account o' how Mac Heggety was ridin' through seems plumb queer.'

'Tommy told me to say if you rode over to the *Laredo Journal* office he'd get the time off.'

'Mighty fine.' He smiled at the girl. 'Shore think it would be great if yuh could ride out, too.'

She lowered her long-lashed eyes. 'I wish I could, but I've got customers who think the store should be open most times. But, Wade, I'd like to thank you for – for – everything!'

'Aw, shucks!' He handed her the paper to pay for the shirt, socks and hat. 'I reckon it's a favour to be helpin' yuh, Stella.'

He left the shop eventually and made his way down the busy street to his hotel. Up in his room, he counted his money. He had not much. Two weeks of living at the Bonanza Hotel and he would be out of dinero. He would have to start earning before that. Maybe he could work a placer somewhere on the river.

He stuck his new fawn hat on but did not use the shirt. It would only gather dust and sweat if he was going to ride out to the canyon. He went to the livery. His black horse was fresh, rested and fed. He slipped the headstall on to the animal and fastened the saddle and cinch while the black rubbed a velvety nose against him. Then he rode out after a word to the hostler.

Wade Tulane found Tommy Camden at the small wood building which served as printing works and office for the *Laredo Journal*. As Wade walked into the printing room, an elderly man who was wearing a green apron glanced up. Wade concluded this was Ben Smith, Tommy's boss and the proprietor of the newspaper.

Tommy came out of a tiny cubby-hole of an office at hearing the sound of Wade's entrance, and soon introductory remarks were made.

'William Camden was a friend o' mine,' said Ben Smith. 'And I for one would like his killers brought to justice. I stand with the sheriff for law and order, Mr Tulane. But I'm also for you – Tommy has told me how you have helped him so far.'

'Maybe he can git the time off to ride with me this mornin'?' suggested Wade.

'Sure, if it's important. We haven't got regular hours here, anyway.'

Tommy Camden went down the street to the drapery store and saddled his horse at the back of the place. Some minutes later the two men rode off, leaving town with a clatter of hooves as they let the horses skim off their freshness.

The trip to the canyon where William Camden had met his death took some time and the seven miles of riding took them through some barren country. They were many miles to the eastern side of the River Shasta. On the ride they saw flowers tucked under the creosote bushes; the inevitable clumps of sage that sent up an aroma when the horses' hooves kicked them. Cacti blossomed in vivid pink and deep red. The desert land was studded with Saguaro cacti, ironwood, mesquite and catclaw clumps. On the ground they frequently saw the queer S-curved tracks of sidewinders. Buzzards and hawks were distant black specks gainst a flawless blue sky. The sun was a molten yellow orb that soon had the horses and men sweating.

Eventually the two riders entered the canyon. The walls rose sheer and fairly tall and were formed of yellow sandstone scoured into queer marking by the winds and rains of hundreds of winters. The canyon bed was flat yellow sand, studded with the inevitable cholla cactus. Halfway down the silent canyon, Tommy reined in his horse and pointed to the wall on his left.

'That's where I saw Mr Mac Heggety snoopin' around!'

Wade stared around. 'Jest a durned canyon! But yuh figgered Mac Heggety was examinin' the canyon wall?'

'He was,' said Tommy eagerly. 'He was lookin' for something. Though what the heck he expected to find has me beat!'

'Where was yore father found dead, Tommy?'

Silently, the youngster urged his horse forward about twenty yards down the canyon and stopped. He was pretty close to the canyon wall.

'About here, Wade. So far as I know. Two ranchers, ridin' through this way, found him and brought him back to town only a few hours after he had been killed.'

Wade looked back along the canyon. Then he stared up at the yellow sandstone wall, at the grooves scoured by the winds and rains.

'Shore have to admit it's queer that Mac Heggety should ride thisaway. If he and his brother killed yore father, why should Mac want to ride through this canyon an' look around like he had lost somethin'? Yuh figger those hellions lost somethin' when they killed yore Paw?'

'I don't think so,' said the youngster slowly. 'I've got a hunch it's something different. Remember, they tried to buy the store some days later – an' then they ransacked the shop and house some time after that when it was obvious we wouldn't sell no matter how high their offer went.'

Wade nodded. 'Those two buzzards were after somethin' – we can see thet. Now I guess Rip will keep on the same trail.'

'He'll want to kill us!' laughed Tommy, a trifle grimly. 'You for crossin' him – and me for killing his rotten brother!'

'I've got a hunch,' said Wade slowly, 'that he won't go gunnin' for yuh until he finds that somethin' he an' his brother were lookin' for. Can't say thet he'll show me the same consideration!' Wade maintained a searching glance at the canyon wall just above his head. 'Say, do I see some queer markings up there or am I gittin' confused with the wind scourings?'

Tommy stared up for a second or two. Then he climbed up in his saddle and stood on the leather – an Indian trick.

'Just as I thought,' he said. 'Looks like Indian markings on the wall but they've been distorted by sand-laden winds over the centuries. Nothin' unusual around here, Wade. Why just a mile past this canyon you can see the City of Ghosts.'

'What in tarnation is thet?'

Tommy laughed boyishly. 'Why, the City of Ghosts is mostly a lot of old caves which were inhabited by some Indians hundreds of years ago. Different from the Indians of today! These old Indians carved homes in the rocks and must have stayed permanently in one place. All you can see now are these caves and remains of rock carvings – pretty much like these marks up on this canyon wall.'

Wade nodded. He took the makings from his shirt pocket and rolled a cigarette. He lit it and blew smoke into the hot air. The deliberate process had given him time to think.

'Yuh got any notion thet Mac Heggety was lookin' at these old Injun carvings when he lamped yuh?' he asked.

Tommy slipped down into his saddle again. 'Yeah, maybe he was.'

'All the same, he came gunnin' for yuh as soon as he saw yuh,' continued Wade. 'Yuh shot in self-defence an' thet ties up thet part of the business.'

Tommy turned to Wade. There was a determined expression on his young face. He sat straight in the saddle, a slim figure in brown pants and red shirt and black hat. He had a gun in the new holster. There was still a bandage under the shirt, but the wound was apparently little more than painful. He was putting up with it.

'You think Mac Heggety was just lookin' at Indian carvings? Not in this canyon because my father had died here?'

Wade expelled more smoke. 'I got a hunch the two things are mebbe tied together. Was yore father ever interested in these Injun markings – or in the old caves of the City of Ghosts?'

Tommy shook his head.

'Can't rightly say that he was. Nope. The old remains of these lost Indian civilisations wasn't much interest to him. Dad was more interested in community work in Laredo.'

Wade turned his horse and glanced along the canyon wall. 'Hows about havin' a fast pasear to this City of Ghosts? Yuh say it ain't more'n a mile away?'

'That's right. But what good will that do?'

'I don't rightly know, son. Jest figger to take a quick look at these durned caves – jest like we're takin' a good looksee at this canyon, huh!'

Tommy nodded and they moved the horses forward. They trotted the animals down the canyon bed.

At that moment the silence of the yellow canyon was shattered by the vicious spang of a rifle bullet!

Wade Tulane felt his new hat tug as if hit by an invisible hand. Only the thong around his chin held the hat in place.

His horse jibbed in fright, and so did Tommy Camden's mount. Then the two animals sprang into full lope, not only spooked by the drygulch bullet but impelled on by the abrupt application of spur rowels!

A second after the horse leaped into flight, another shot rang. The slug whistled close to Wade Tulane, but he was crouched flat against his black horse. The drygulcher had scored two near misses. The third shot would be unlikely to find a human target for the two horses were taking the riders out of range at a terrific lick.

Wade Tulane had a good idea who wanted to kill him. Rip Heggety! So the galoot had tailed them out to this canyon! Mighty queer that the canyon had already seen two deaths. Seemed like Rip had figured on adding a third!

The marksman had shot from the top of the

canyon wall, over on the right. He'd used a rifle – probably a Winchester. And Wade had noted the two bullets had been trained on him! Rip had not shot at Tommy Camden.

The thud of horses' hooves on the canyon bed lasted for a few minutes and the two riders rapidly put distance between themselves and the drygulcher. Wade Tulane suddenly jerked his mount into the shelter of a huddle of huge boulders. These lay at the end of the canyon, where the canyon walls broke down into scattered rocks and the ground levelled into a flat, cholla-studded basin.

Tommy Camden jigged his pony in beside the other man. He calmed the animal while Wade Tulane dismounted and hitched his horse's ribbons to a spur of rock.

'Ain't no call to allow the gent to do his fancy shootin' an' get away with it!' Wade slipped off his new hat. 'Damned if he ain't shot a hole in it!'

Grimly replacing the headgear, he grabbed at a Colt and then began to climb the huddle of boulders that led to the top of the canyon wall. He slid forward on his stomach when he reached the top part of the high ground. He stared across the canyon and tried to find sign of the drygulcher.

For some moments there was nothing unusual about the arid scene. Silence once more brooded over the terrain. Then Wade's keen, dark eyes saw the figure of a man moving cautiously through rocky cracks on the top of the canyon wall. Momentarily, the diminutive shape of the man showed and then he scrambled out of sight.

The range was too far for a Colt by a long way. Wade got the impression the man was leaving his vantage point now that his attempt to drygulch had failed. Probably the man would be going for his horse. Wade could not be sure that the man was Rip Heggety but he felt this was his handiwork.

Wade Tulane scrambled down quickly to Tommy Camden.

'Thet galoot is on the other side o' the canyon an' goin' for his hoss. If we dash over now, he can't see us goin' over the canyon bed because he's forkin' his bronc. Let's go – on foot. We can git among the rocks where the hosses can't go, and mebbe give him a hot time.'

The invitation to gun-play seemed to delight Tommy Camden and he went off with Wade as fast as their legs could take them across the canyon floor. They hit the first pileup of boulders and then, guns in hands, began slithering through the cracks and gullies formed by the rocks. Soon they were high on the canyon wall, making a way from boulder to boulder and keeping a sharp lookout for the drygulcher. Wade Tulane led the approach, mostly because he was well-versed in the ways of lawless *hombres* and Tommy was not.

Wade knew they could be walking into grief for it was not possible to ascertain where the would-be drygulcher was now. But it was a chance that had to be taken.

As he was moving ahead of Tommy Camden, he suddenly saw Rip Heggety first. Wade looked down from the shelter of a crevice and saw the man below him, busy unhitching a roan that had been hidden in a nook among the rocks.

Unfortunately, Rip Heggety heard or sensed movement above him almost at the same time that Wade saw him. He dived for cover like some startled animal.

Wade's shot bit into rock inches from the man. Rip Heggety had found cover just a second to the good. The crack of the gun spooked the roan and it kicked its legs and ran down the narrow defile among the rocks. The defile twisted so abruptly that the horse was out of sight in seconds.

Then a shot spat out of the rocks and the slug hissed at Wade Tulane. He ducked instinctively. He heard a clatter of boots on rock just below him. He knew Rip Heggety was moving away. Wade shot a glance from out of cover in the hope the other man would provide a target. The scraping of boots on rock came to his ears but there was no sign of Rip Heggety. He was moving through the cracks between the confused pileup of boulders.

Wade snapped off another slug at the huddle of rocks below him and he moved to another advantage point, hoping to get a sight of Rip Heggety. But it was not to be. The man was still moving in the cover of the crevices between the rocks. In some places he was evidently squirming through like a rattler! But he kept his head down. In fact, there was no sign of him, even when Wade Tulane shifted position once more.

And then, suddenly, Wade heard the sound of hoofbeats on loose stones and rock and knew that Rip Heggety had got to his horse and was moving off. The clatter lasted a few seconds. Wade stood up; leaped to a point of rock, gun in hand and tried to get a view of the fleeing rider.

When he did see the man it was only momentary and his snapped-off shot was just that split-second late. Rip Heggety was rowelling the roan through a narrow defile, pushing through catclaw that almost chocked the crack. Then, as the shot rang out after him, he turned the jerking horse around another twist in the defile and was lost to Wade's view.

7

SUCCESSFUL
SEARCH

The next view of Rip Heggety was as a distant figure
on a galloping horse. They were going over the
barren ground at the end of the canyon. Wade stood
up and stared. Then he turned and tapped Tommy
Camden on the arm.

'C'mon, let's fork the hosses!'

They scrambled down the heaped-up masses of
broken rock and then raced across the canyon floor.
But by the time they got the horses it was obvious Rip
Heggety had crossed the basin of flat land and was
now riding through the broken terrain beyond.
Wade and Tommy sent their horses full lope across
the arid basin and then pulled up as they encountered the numerous shale gullies. Rip Heggety could
have taken any one of these paths.

'Wal, looks like he lights out mighty fast when things don't go as he plans,' drawled Wade.

'He must have been trailin' us,' commented Tommy. 'Maybe he saw us leave town. The drygulch skunk!'

'It was me who he sighted his shells on,' said Wade dryly. 'Shore confirms my hunch thet he ain't gunnin' for yuh, young feller, until he gits what he was lookin' for at yore store.'

'But we haven't anythin' of interest to Rip Heggety at our store – or the house!' snapped Tommy.

'Must be some durned thing or those two galoots wouldn't ha' been so mighty keen to buy yuh up!'

'Wade – that jasper has rode off but he'll try again! Gosh, I feel we've dragged you into this!'

Wade Tulane grinned. 'Forget it. I've tangled with thet cuss now an' there ain't no goin' back.'

They continued the ride. They had intended to visit the City of Ghosts and they saw no reason why the gun-play should deter them. They rode with guns in hands, however. Wade looked warily around, the taut, unsmiling expression back on his face. Tommy Camden led the way through a gully which eventually led to another strech of flat land. Across this area of heat-hazed land was the rocky wall of a high mesa. They rode across the ground at full lope and then, close to the cliff, stopped to blow the horses.

'This is the City of Ghosts,' explained Tommy. 'See those cave mouths and the carvings above that ledge? Guess it must be hundreds of years old. Those ancient Indians had a civilisation of sorts, by all the tales I've heard. If you care to look in the caves you'll see more carved images and pillars and arches. Yeah, that cliff face is really the remains of an old, old city.'

'Those carvings link up with the marks in the canyon,' muttered Wade Tulane. 'Queer!'

'You want a closer looksee into those caves?' asked Tommy.

'What the heck good will thet do?' countered Wade Tulane. 'Mebbe this old site connects with the canyon where yore Dad was killed, but I don't see much point to it all. Jest this similarity of old Injun markings. Mebbe thet don't mean a thing, anyway! Wal, guess we've seen all we want to see – the canyon an' this place.'

And with a last searching glance at the silent, brooding caves in the mesa face, Wade turned his horse. They rode back through the canyon of death – the place where William Camden and Mac Heggety had died. Then they trotted the horses out of the other end. The ride back to Laredo started, and they took pretty much the same sort of trail back. It was when they were still two miles out of the town and on the rutted trail that swept through the Shasta valley, that they saw the sheriff, Bill Hapner. He was riding a puffing bronc slowly along the trail. Tommy and Wade came alongside him.

'Howdy, Sheriff,' said Wade, 'yuh been chasin' someone? Yore nag is shore blowin'.'

'You don't miss much,' grunted the other. 'Yep, I been ridin' fast after a galoot but he tricked me goin' through the mesquite bushes.'

'We've been shot at by Rip Heggety!' Tommy blurted out. 'I showed Wade the canyon where my Dad was killed, an' then guns started poppin'!'

'Wal, what yuh want me to do?' barked the sheriff. 'The way things are around here jest now I can't go around warnin' every doggone gunslinger to quit disturbin' the peace!' The sheriff shot a last disgruntled glance along the trail. 'I'm ridin' back to town. Yuh ridin' along with me?'

It was a slow ride back because the sheriff's mount was winded. Wade Tulane took time off to examine his hat and sorrowfully shake his head over the bullet hole in it. It seemed his hats were fated to suffer in Laredo!

They rode into town and halted outside the sheriff's office as Bill Hapner hitched his horse to the tie-rail. As Wade and Tommy sat in their saddles another man rode up. He was Dave Latimer and his honest face was lit up with a smile. He rode his bay close up to Wade Tulane and the young fellow, and then hailed Sheriff Hapner.

'Howdy, folks! This is shore a grand mornin' for me! Just made a deal with the railroad company 'bout shipping my beef. Say, railroading cattle is better than a slow trail-herd!'

Dave Latimer dismounted. He stepped to the boardwalk outside the sheriff's office. He turned to Wade and Tommy.

'Say, C'mon inside Bill's office an' have a parley. Bill won't mind – that right, yuh old badge-toter?'

'Shore, use my office as a goldarn saloon!' barked the other.

Dave Latimer laughed uproariously. 'Never mind him! C'mon, I'd like to hear the news. There's lots I'd like to hear about yuh, Tommy!'

Tommy Camden got down from his horse. He led it to the tie-rail and hitched the reins.

'All right, guess I've got ten minutes more to waste. I'd like to tell you, Mr Latimer, how Wade has helped me.'

'Jest moseying around —' began Wade.

'We're tryin' to find out why the Heggety brothers wanted to buy our store,' interposed Tommy.

Dave Latimer nodded. 'Shore, shore! C'mon inside this old John Law's office and sit down an' chat.'

Wade dismounted, and good-humouredly, went inside the office with the others. They managed to find seats but Wade Tulane found himself beside Bill Hapner's desk. The sheriff brought out his carefully-hoarded bottle of whisky and poured three glasses.

'Reckon yuh ain't qualified to drink whisky, young feller,' he barked at Tommy Camden. 'And I ain't the one to start yuh!'

Tommy blinked and looked a little peeved. For the hundredth time lately he wished he had another two years on his tally. He was at a bad age, he figured. Men like Bill Hapner reckoned he was still a kid!

There was five minutes of general discussion, which enlightened Dave Latimer considerably with regard to Rip Heggety and his activities.

Bill Hapner was the hardy, restless type who could not sit at a desk very long. He got up and went to the window and stared at the street-scene. A stage was waiting outside a hotel. At a word from Bill Hapner, Dave Latimer joined him and together they watched some passengers collect around the stage, preparatory to boarding for their journey. It seemed that Bill Hapner and Dave Latimer knew the passengers and were interested in their activities.

Wade Tulane was not very much concerned with the personalities of Laredo – except those who affected him at the moment. He stayed in his seat beside the desk and smoked. Tommy Camden got up and crossed to the window. The three of them seemed to be very interested in the people departing by stage that morning.

At that moment Bill Hapner's deputy entered the

office and slapped a large envelope down on the desk. Then he picked it up again and slit it open.

'Been to the post office,' he said cordially to Wade. 'Ain't nothing much 'cept another consignment o' Wanted notices. Plenty o' them these days!'

The deputy did not see the line in Wade's face stiffen. The man was too busy leafing through a number of sheets which were pinned together. He flipped through the papers casually. Wade let his cigarette smoulder in his hand.

The deputy hardly looked at the sheets. He was about to slip them back into the big envelope when a hail came from Bill Hapner.

'Hey, Chad, c'mon over here an' see who's leavin' on the stage with the Fenton widow!'

The deputy joined the others at the window. Wade stared at the pinned sheets. Then he reached out a hand. He kept flicking narrow glances at the others at the window.

'Seems like the stage will have to fold up bizness afore long,' chuckled Dave Latimer.

'Thet ain't so,' drawled Bill Hapner. 'Folks don't always trust railroads. What if them cars come off the rails at thet terrible speed – nigh on twenty-five miles an hour! Huh!'

'The railroad for me,' said Tommy eagerly.

'As for me, I do my travellin' on my hoss,' said the deputy.

Wade Tulane leafed silently through the Wanted notices. He scanned them grimly, intently, one by one. He flicked a glance at the men at the window. They were deriving some amusement in watching the stage. The departure of people in a town like Laredo was always interesting.

Wade Tulane halted at one sheet and his lips thinned to a tight line.

His name stared up at him! But no picture!

He worked swiftly and silently after that, wasting not another second. His fingers slipped the pin out. He detached the wanted sheet and then pinned the other notices together again. He silently folded the sheet that bore his name. He never took his eyes off others at the window while his fingers silently worked. He slipped the sheet into his shirt pocket. Then he dropped his eyes to the wanted sheets again.

At that moment Sheriff Hapner turned, an amused grin on his lips. It did not alter as he came to Wade; not even when he realized Wade had been looking at the Wanted posters.

'Heck, yuh interested in them outlaws?'

'Sometimes a man can pick up bounty money,' said Wade gravely.

'Yep, an' sometimes git a slug in his guts for his trouble,' grunted the other.

The deputy turned. 'Those notices jest came in, Bill.'

'Yeah. I guessed that. Knew yuh'd been out for the mail.'

Sheriff Bill Hapner glanced through the sheets and shook his head in disgust. He opened a drawer and pushed the notices inside.

'I'll study 'em when I feel like it. I could cover the wall outside with these doggone Wanted notices! I guess I'll pin some of 'em up on the cottonwoods outside the town. That'll give some target practice to some ornery galoot.'

Wade got to his feet. 'Mebbe we ought to be movin', Tommy. I got a feelin' we ought to look over yore store and try figger out why the Heggety brothers were so mighty keen to buy yuh up – that's if yuh want me nosin' around?'

'Why, sure, Wade,' said Tommy warmly. 'Yuh can poke around all day if it'll explain why those galoots ransacked the house and store.'

'Maybe I can help, too' said Dave Latimer.

'Yep. Stella will be pleased to see you, Mr Latimer.'

On this note they left the sheriff and his deputy to their routine business. Wade rode along in silence with the other two. They let the horses walk down the dusty street until the drapery store was reached and there they hitched up the animals to a convenient rail. Stella Camden was busy serving two old customers when they walked through the store to the living-quarters at the back. She could not leave her customers, who were two women bent on combining gossip with their shopping. Tommy Camden showed Wade and Dave Latimer into the living-room and indicated chairs.

'Don't know thet we should be sittin' around,' murmured Wade. He glanced around the comfortable room. His eyes alighted on a bureau. Thoughtfully, he turned to Tommy. 'Yuh been through all yore father's effects since his death?'

The young fellow followed Wade's glance to the bureau.

'Sure. We had to check through everythin' when Stella decided to keep on runnin' the business.'

'Yuh didn't find anythin' that might interest two tough *hombres* like the Heggety brothers?'

'Nothing, I guess. Dad never had any truck with those jaspers to the best of my knowledge. Nope. Just wasn't anything to connect with them.'

'And I guess yuh didn't find anythin' else of unusual interest – I mean somethin' out of the ordinary – somethin' yore Dad wouldn't be usually mixed up in?'

Tommy shook his head slowly, eyes fixed thoughtfully on the Indian rug.

'Just wasn't anythin' unusual, Wade. Oh, I've thought about it on those lines since those two jaspers ransacked the house.'

Wade nodded. 'I guess yuh would, son. Jest goin' over the facts, that's all. Was thet bureau ransacked?'

'Yeah, how did you guess?'

Wade smiled. 'I've a hunch it was yore Paw's – thet right?'

'Yeah. Sure, it was open and the papers messed around – but nothin' was missing. That's the queer part. Nothin' was missin' from the house or store that we could see.'

'They didn't rob yuh of anythin'?'

'Nope. There was some money in the store till. Could have taken that, but they didn't.'

Wade nodded. 'I'm convinced they were lookin' for somethin' that was hidden by yore father. That somethin' is still probably hidden. Mac and Rip Heggety started out by wantin' to buy the premises – probably reckonin' thet it was the easiest way to find this somethin'. When yuh refused to sell, they took a chance on ransacking the place.'

'Those two birds were not exactly gentle,' remarked Dave Latimer. 'I reckon they didn't find what they wanted. Particularly as Tommy and Stella caught them at it. Can't get a notion o' what they want though!'

Wade glanced around again. 'There's somethin' hidden in this house,' he said quietly. 'I've got a hunch yore father hid it an' Rip Heggety knows what it is.'

'But he doesn't know where to find it,' supplied Tommy.

Wade walked around the living-room and nodded in confirmation of the other's remark. He looked at the clapboard walls and at the stone fireplace. There was a high mantelpiece on which stood many little ornaments and Indian carvings. Two old shotguns were fastened to a wall in cross-wise fashion.

'Did yuh ever look in out-of-way places when yuh checked yore father's effects?' asked Wade.

'You mean hiding-places?' Tommy shook his head. 'Wal, nope. Dad wasn't the man to hide things, anyway. He was a tidy man. But if yuh want to start a search, Wade, by all means let us look.'

'That's what I was gettin' at,' admitted Wade Tulane. 'Let's have a look inside thet chimney, for a start, huh? Never can tell. Those Heggety jaspers must ha' been lookin' for somethin'!'

The three men were nothing loath to start something which might help solve the mysteries, and they began by inspecting the inside of the wide chimney. At this time of the year, there was no fire. Although Wade dislodged some soot in his inspection, there was nothing else. Then he realized the Heggety brothers must have looked into the stone chimney during the occosion of their unlawful search. Wade turned away and tested the floorboards of the living-room. He tapped with his foot at various parts, although Indian rugs covered a great deal of the floor. Tommy and Dave Latimer were examining

110

some of the beams of the roof. While they were all at work, Stella Camden entered the room, having got rid of her customers.

'Well, what goes on?' she wanted to know.

'A search, sis,' Tommy said quickly. 'We're tryin' to find whatever the Heggety jaspers were tryin' to find!'

'Well, that's a good idea. How about the bedrooms and the kitchen?'

After some minutes the search became a matter for silent, determined work. Wade took up the rugs – with Stella's permission! Tommy went into his bedroom and began looking into nooks and corners where he had never thought of looking. Dave Latimer actually went outside the premises, to the stable, and made a search there.

Stella looked around her bedroom. If there was any reason for the Heggety brothers' ransacking, they were determined to find it.

Even as he worked, Wade Tulane realized Mac and Rip Hegety could have been ransacking the house on false assumptions. On the other hand, there might be something very definite to be discovered.

Wade tested the flooring. Most of it seemed very secure, but there was a part which moved under his boots. A loose board, no less. He used a poker on the task of getting the board up. He was well aware that many old timers favoured the space under floorboards as a hiding-place and so it was a good bet to take a look-see under the floor. Anyway, if they searched the house in this way and still found nothing, it would at least eliminate one factor.

The board was not difficult to get up, he needed the poker only as an initial means of getting the board raised an inch. He wondered why it was slack when all the rest of the planks were very secure. This bit of board was only about a foot long.

Wade thrust a hand into the space below and felt around very cautiously. His hand rasped a joist. There was a drop of about eighteen inches to bare earth. He sank his arm into the hole and felt around. Nothing that could vaguely be termed interesting met his touch. It seemed like his efforts were futile. He drew his hand up again and only as a last measure felt along the underside of the nearest bit of flooring. The pine boards were rough to his hands – he was about to draw back with a muttered word of disgust when his fingers lightly touched something that swung under the movement of his hand.

He soon realized it was a small leather bag tied to a nail. He pulled it away; stared at it and knew this must surely be what they were seeking. He had swift impressions; the little soft leather bag was light; almost seemed empty.

Then he gave a shout to the others. It brought them running. Wade stood up.

'I've found somethin',' he said quietly. 'A little leather bag tied to a nail on the underside of this cavity. Did yuh know it was here, Tommy?'

'Heck, no! D'you think this is —'

'Looks like this is what Rip Heggety wants,' said Wade. 'If yuh know nothin' about it, looks like yore Paw hid it under there.' Wade suddenly handed the soft leather bag to Tommy Camden. 'It's yore's, son.'

Tommy accepted the bag wonderingly. 'I don't get it,' he faltered. 'Why the heck should Dad hide this? I wonder what it's all about? Gosh, I'd better open the bag!'

He slackened the string and opened the small bag of leather. Then a moment later he took out the contents. It was a sheet of paper which had been carefully folded into a square about three inches by three. Tommy slowly unfolded the paper and then stared at it.

'It's a map!' he gulped.

Slowly, he turned and went to the table and smoothed the paper down to the flat surface. Wade was stamping the board into place again when Tommy called the others around him.

'Look at it! What do yuh make of it, Wade? It's done in pencil – and it looks like my Dad's work! Look at that writing, Stella! Dad made this drawing.' They crowded around. Dave Latimer came into the room and joined them. They stared at the map.

'Looks mighty like a map of a canyon,' said Wade slowly. 'Carefully done, too. See these instructions! Shows anyone how to locate the place from Laredo.'

'Good heavens, it's a map of the canyon where William Camden was found dead!' exclaimed Dave Latimer.

On the bottom of the sheet was some wording which ran as follows:

'Siomi Indian caves. Main entrance located as per map. Note Indian markings on canyon wall. Rock falls have completely closed the caves. The gold has been buried for centuries. It can be left until I decide what to do.'

In utter silence the party of four scanned the words and stared at the fatal map. The whole thing sank into the minds of those present.

Gold!

That was what the Heggety brothers were after! Probably that was why they had killed William Camden, although the details that had led to the killing were not quite clear.

'I don't understand – how – how Dad got this map – or – how he knew about this gold!' gasped Stella. 'He wasn't a gold hunter.'

'You can put it another way, sis,' added Tommy. 'He was against the gold fever. He didn't like the lawlessness it was bringin' to Laredo.'

'Then how – how – did he learn about these caves?'

'That's a little mystery which I reckon will come out into the light o' day sooner or later,' said Wade, and he moved away from the table. Just to look at the sheet of paper, reminded him of the damning Wanted poster in his shirt pocket. He would have to burn it at the earliest opportunity.

'Now yuh know why Rip and Mac Heggety wanted to buy yuh up,' exclaimed Dave Latimer. 'So they knew about this gold! Jest their meat! Gold! They knew Wiliam had this map. It's all comin' clear. If we could only prove that they shot yore father, we might swing thet hellion Rip Heggety on a cottonwood limb!'

'We'll get around to thet, mebbe,' said Wade grimly. Tommy Camden grabbed at the map and swung impulsively to Wade Tulane.

'Let's ride out to thet canyon an' see if we can locate these caves! Why, this map shows the same spot in the canyon where we were lookin' just this morn! It all adds up. There must be an old hidden cave in that canyon! Looks like it's relic of the old lost tribe of Indians! Can't say I've ever heard of any living Siomi Injuns!'

'Nor me, either!' contributed Dave Latimer.

Wade swung again. 'Jest take it easy, young feller. Yuh want us to go tearin' out there with pick an' shovel?'

'Wal, if there's gold—'

'There's also Rip Heggety an' he wants this gold. He also hankers to kill me, an' I figger he'll kill yuh as soon as he grabs thet map. Although yuh salivated his brother, I figger he's laid off you because he thought mebbe yuh might know somethin' about this gold or the map.'

'Gosh, I'm not scared of that sidewinder!' began the young man.

'Nope. I know thet. But jest take it easy. Yore father wasn't in any hurry to go digging for thet cave.'

'You mean we shouldn't do anythin' about it at all?' demanded the youngster.

Wade grinned at the other's indignation. 'I don't mean that, Tommy. Matter o' fact, the responsibility is yours – I reckon it's yore map, left to yuh by yore Dad. But take it easy. I figger Rip Heggety will do murder to get this map!'

'Wade's right,' supplied Dave Latimer. 'In fact, this discovery is purty close to dynamite.'

'I tell you what,' said Stella quickly. 'Let's have something to eat and we can discuss what we'll do. Thanks to you, Wade, we've at least achieved something.'

'Aw, shucks, yuh'd have gotten around to searching the place yoreself,' muttered Wade.

But Stella Camden was determined that the men should have a good meal and she set to work in the

116

kitchen. Tommy had to go out to attend a customer who entered the store. Later, over the meal, the girl learned about the shooting at the canyon and how they had inspected the City of Ghosts.

Then they made plans to ride out and inspect the canyon again with a view to finding the entrance to the old Siomi Indian caves.

Dave Latimer volunteered to help Tommy and Wade. They went out to the horses and led them around to the stable at the back and there slung two picks and two shovels around the saddles.

Stella Camden had to stay behind. It was really a bad decision.

8

DIRTY MOVES

Leo Sand watched the three riders leave town. He
stood on a boardwalk, smoking a cigarette, and
stared at Wade Tulane as he rode past. His pale face
twisted in a sneer. His brain juggled with many
thoughts, and he wondered where the three were
heading. Then he noticed the picks and shovels, and
another sneer crossed his face. Were these lot adding
to the mugs working the placers on the river?

If that was the case, Rip Heggety might like to
know about it!

Leo Sand turned away, throwing his brown-paper
cigarette to the dusty roadway. He figured he would
get his horse and take a pasear.

Maybe this was a chance for Rip Heggety to even
with Wade Tulane and Tommy Camden. Rip sure
hated Tulane, and Tommy Camden had killed Mac

119

Heggety. If Rip Heggety could get around to throwing lead, he might eliminate those two. In fact, if he salivated Dave Latimer in the process, all better. The rancher was too blamed bossy where Stella Camden was concerned. With him out of the way, the setup would be even more improved.

Leo Sand went to his livery, motivated by his inbitten thoughts.

He got his cayuse out and rode out of town. He naturally took the trail to the placer workings. He caught up with Wade Tulane, Dave Latimer and Tommy Camden – at least he saw them fork off the trail where one track led to the river and the other out over the desert. Leo Sand stared at the disappearing riders. So they were not going to the placer camp! Why, then, were they carrying picks and shovels?

He didn't get it, but he realized they were taking the desert trail. Rip Heggety might like to learn about this!

If Rip wanted to, he could hit the saddle and take his hoglegs along to a shooting match when he caught up with the three riders. Heggety had pals, so he shouldn't be lost for extra guns if he figured they were needed.

Leo Sand rowelled his horse again. One thing, the others three riders had not seen him!

And other thing – which was very interesting –

Stella Camden must have been left behind in Laredo! And without the three men who were sworn to protect her! Very interesting!

He'd ride to the placer camp – then, maybe, he'd ride back to town and pay the girl a visit.

In the meantime, the three riders jogged along at a moderate lope, the sort of pace the horses could maintain all day if necessary. The seven miles to the canyon did not make for a long ride. They got there without really hurrying the animals.

Eventually they cantered into the canyon, the horses avoiding the clumps of cactus and the old, weird Joshua trees. Then they rode up to the canyon wall where the strange old Indian markings were visible. The three men stared at the hieroglyphics, not that they made much sense. The winds and rains of centuries had scoured them and only a scholar could decipher them.

Wade Tulane said: 'This is where you git thet map out, Tommy! Seems like there ought to be an entrance to a cave somewhere around hyar.'

Tommy got the map out eagerly; flattened it against his saddle. 'Gosh, I'd like to find gold!'

'Reckon it brings grief,' said Dave Latimer slowly. 'Yore Paw knew that judging by the way he hid this map.'

'That's somethin' that we've got to figure out,' commented Wade as he stared around the silent

canyon. 'How'd yore father git that map? You don't
know the answer, Tommy. But we'll maybe find out
sooner or later. And another thing – how come he
was sure there'd be gold in these lost caves?'

'Bit of a mystery,' muttered Dave Latimer. 'But we
ain't worrying about it now, Wade. Maybe we'll find
out an' maybe we won't. The main job is to locate
these darned Injun caves.'

'Yep.' Wade stared along the canyon wall and at
the scoured marking again. 'Accordin' to the map we
got to note the Injun markings. Wal, we shore have
noted 'em. You see any sign of a cave, Tommy?'

'Not a thing,' confessed the young man. 'But goin'
by the map the mouth should be about there.' And
Tommy Camden pointed to a spot just left of the
scoured Indian hieroglyphics. The three men stared,
silent and thoughtful. The canyon wall seemed solid,
although it was very jagged and bore a bit of a slope
on which wind-scoured rocks lay heaped.

Then Wade Tulane laughed curtly. 'We shore got a
job on hand, fellers. Looks like we oughta git down
from the saddle and start digging. Looks like a
mighty lot of rock might have to be shifted.'

'We might be lucky and strike through to the cave
quickly,' responded Tommy.

Wade and Dave Latimer exchanged grins. The
eagerness of the young reporter was refreshing if
somewhat optimistic.

Still, he might be right at that. The apparently solid heap of jagged rock might – and should if the map was accurate – hide a cave, an age-old cave used by the Siomi Indians.

They threw the reins over the horses' heads, thus ground-hitching them, and unloaded the digging gear. Wade took a drink of water from his canteen. The afternoon sun was still fierce and a drink before starting work seemed a great idea.

Dave, Tommy and Wade grabbed at picks and shovels and started on the approximate spot indicated by the map as the mouth of the old cave. The first chore was to prise away a big boulder. This was a matter for the three of them using shovels and picks.

'Reckon that rock has bin there since the white man came to this durned country,' grunted Dave Latimer when the boulder was finaly rolled clear.

'Yep. An' we still got a heap o' work afore we make even a dint in this rock,' grunted Wade Tulane.

'Let's really hit it!' exclaimed Tommy, and he attacked the heaped rocks with great energy.

'Kinda hot work with this blamed sun,' remarked Wade. 'I got a notion this work should be done at night.'

'I guess that would waste time!' commented Tommy as he heaved on his pick.

'Not so shore about that.' Wade straightened his back and looked around him. 'Don't forget, Rip

Heggety is interested in this canyon. The moment he learns we're digging, he'll be mighty keen to take over.'

'We wouldn't let that happen.'

'Guess not. Jest that that *hombre* has some hardy characters riding herd with him an' he might figure to force an issue.'

Dave Latimer quit digging for a moment. 'You really mean that, Wade? About digging at night?'

'Jest an idea,' muttered the other. 'You'll allow there'll be Colt lead the minnit Rip Heggety spots us at work – an' that *hombre* will be along this way sooner or later. I can't see us gittin' the cave mouth cleared without hours of work an' all that time Heggety has a chance to ride up thisaway.'

'Let him ride up!' snapped Tommy. 'I'd like a chance to swap lead with that *hombre*!'

'Yuh talk real war-talk, young feller,' grinned Wade Tulane. 'But let's git on with the diggin'. I reckon we might just as well git on with it.'

'Yep. To blazes with that Rip Heggety hellion!' retorted Dave Latimer.

While they were talking they little realized that Leo Sand had met up with Rip Heggety at the placer camp and had talked to good effect. So much that the snarling Rip Heggety had called Dutch from the placer and told him to get the horses.

'Yuh say those fellers had picks and shovels, Mister Sand?'

'Yep. Went out by the desert trail.'

'Yeah?' Rip Heggety fingered his unshaven face and looked thoughtful. 'Wal, thanks for the tally. Me an' Dutch will take the trail.'

'Kill them,' said Leo Sand softly. 'Remember, Tommy Camden shot yore brother.'

'Yuh still hankerin' for thet gal!' sneered Rip Heggety. 'Hell, iffen I wanted a gal I'd jest carry her off!'

'Every man to his own way,' said Leo Sand smoothly. 'Got any idea why those three *hombres* have ridden out with picks and shovels?'

'I got ideas,' gritted the other. 'Outa my way, feller! Hey, Dutch – yuh goin' to be all day with them horses!'

'Just about ready!' rumbled Dutch, and he yanked on the cinch of his own big mare.

Leo Sand rode out of the placer camp well satisfied with the trend of events. He had no doubt that Rip Heggety and his pard, Dutch, would catch up with Wade Tulane, Tommy Camden and Dave Latimer, the rancher. And after that Colt lead should fly. He hoped the three men who stood between him and Stella would hit the dust and stay there.

He rode into town, went into a saloon to down a quick drink of redeye and then came out again and continued to Stella's drapery store. He hitched his horse at the tie-rail. He went up to the boardwalk, entered the emporium.

Stella came to the counter and stopped dead on seeing Leo Sand. 'You!'

'Me!' grinned the gambler. 'Jest figured to pay a visit, Stella!'

'Please – I don't want to see you!'

'That ain't no way to speak to me,' snapped Leo Sand.

'Please don't make this unpleasant,' breathed the girl. 'You know I don't want your attentions. Now please go.'

'Not so durned quick,' snapped Leo Sand, mad to think that this girl should spurn him. 'I know your brother an' that pesky Wade Talune are not around. They rode out o' town with thet rancher feller, Dave Latimer.'

'Oh – you saw them – that's why you're here!' whispered the girl, and she instinctively backed.

'Figured to talk to you alone,' said the gambler harshly. 'You know I want to marry you, Stella. I want to be an important man in this town an' I reckon a girl like you would kinda give me background.'

'You – a tinhorn gambler!' Contempt was in her voice. 'I don't want to marry you – can't you get that straight?'

Rage filled Leo Sand's voice. 'Yuh got eyes for that blamed stranger, Wade Tulane.'

'That's – that's not for you to say!' flared the girl, a flush on her cheeks.

126

'I know it. Wal, he'll get his,' said the man evilly, 'The whole blamed issue will get a bellyful of lead – I – ah —'

Even Leo Sand knew he had said too much in his anger. Stella's eyes widened in horror.

'You saw them ride out and – and – oh, you know something!'

'Forget it!' snarled the man.

'They're ridin' into a trap,' breathed the girl, instinct supplying the answer if not the details.

'You're crazy, girl!' grated Leo Sand. 'I never said that.'

'But it's true! I can guess it!' And Stella, hardly knowing more than this sure hunch, turned and ran into the living-quarters at the back of the store.

She had in mind to saddle her horse and ride out after her brother and Wade Tulane and Dave Latimer. Goaded into actions he knew were blundering, Leo Sand followed the girl into the house. He grabbed her and held her. It was the first time he had ever held the girl in his arms and the sensation aroused everything savage in him. Stella struggled and gave a sharp scream.

'Cut it out!' snapped the man. 'That won't do yuh any good. And don't fight me – just say yuh'll be mine!'

'No!'

'Yuh'll be mighty glad to turn to me when yuh're

all alone!' snarled Leo Sand. 'Guess yuh'll need a man then, my girl!'

'Then it's right,' breathed the girl. 'You expect Wade, Tommy and Mr Latimer to be killed! Oh, heavens, I must warn them! Let me go!'

The struggle began in real earnest. Leo Sand knew he had made admissions that might be troublesome but, on second thoughts, he was sure a few fool words didn't matter. When the three who had ridden into the desert were dead, words wouldn't be of much account.

He didn't intend to let the girl go running out of the store. In fact, he wanted to bend her to his will. He would show her who was master!

But Stella Camden was strong and possessed with righteous anger at this man pawing her. She struck his face and pushed. It was more by accident that Leo Sand stumbled, but Stella's resistance had helped. She quickly ran from the room, getting away from his grasp with a fast movement. She rushed out into the yard at the back and then into the street.

9

MAN DOWN

Stella Camden ran instinctively to the sheriff's office and with every yard she covered she blessed her luck in escaping from Leo Sand. She would complain to the sheriff. Bill Hapner would know how to deal with the young gambler.

Leo Sand saw the girl head for the sheriff's office and he cursed his luck. He halted on the boardwalk outside the drapery store; then he swung around and grabbed at his horse. He figured to get out. He realized he had made a fool play in approaching Stella Camden. He didn't want to explain his actions to the sheriff of Laredo. Far better to light out and hope that events in the desert would go the way he wanted.

By the time Stella found Bill Hapner and poured out her fears to him, Leo Sand had rode out of town. But he had no intention of riding to the desert!

Gunplay was not his line. He did not want to ride until he met up with Rip Heggety and Dutch; on the contrary he'd lie low and hope that some of his enemies would die of lead poisoning.

Stella grabbed Bill Hapner's arm. 'Leo Sand has been pestering me! But worse than that he gave me a hint that Tommy and Wade Tulane and Dave Latimer are ridin' into a trap.'

'Huh? Where they gone?' grunted the sheriff.

'They're ridin' out to the canyon where my father was killed. We made a discovery in the house. There's hidden gold in that canyon, Sheriff!'

'Gold!' he ejaculated. 'Wal, there's always grief whar there's gold! Whar's this pesky Leo Sand? I'll kick his hide!'

And Bill Hapner stamped into the street with the girl, but the gambler had vanished. He returned to the drapery store with the girl. She began locking up while the sheriff stared grimly up and down the street in case Leo Sand had not gone far. Then Stella went to the stables at the back of the house and led out her horse.

'I'm ridin' out after Tommy, Wade Tulane and Mr Latimer,' she said. 'I reckon to warn them.'

'Jest hold it, Miss Stella!' barked the sheriff. 'I can't jest allow yuh to ride alone iffen there's danger. I'll mosey along with yuh. Give me a chance to git my hoss. An' I guess yuh can explain more as we take the trail, huh?'

Despite her fears, Stella smiled. 'Thanks, Sheriff. But we must hurry! I'm afraid! I must warn Tommy and the others that there is some sort of danger.'

'Reckon them three *hombres* can tackle danger as it comes,' said Sheriff Hapner dryly. 'But I'll ride along wi' yuh – I want to know more about this!'

He did not waste much time in saddling his horse and joining the girl in the dusty street. Then, with a final glance around for sign of Leo Sand, he rode along with the girl.

On the ride she told the sheriff about the finding of the map showing the whereabouts of the long-lost cave in the canyon. Stella thought it best to tell the sheriff everything Then, the brief facts told, they urged the horses into a fast lope. Soon they were heading into the desert terrain.

In the meantime, Wade Tulane and the others were making good progress towards uncovering the cave mouth. They had rolled several large boulders to one side, boulders that had lain in position for hundreds of years. They considered that they were right on the cave mouth.

And then it happened. A shot cracked through the silent canyon and sent a burst of dust up near Wade's feet. He didn't need to be told the shell came from a rifle. He didn't need anyone to tell him to dive for cover. In fact, all three men darted to the large boulders that had been levered out of the cave mouth.

131

They found they made excellent cover!

'Wonder who them varmints are!' snorted Wade.

'I don't need to guess!' yelled Tommy. 'Rip Heggety! And maybe a pal or two! Who else?'

'You said it, Tommy,' returned Wade. 'Heggety! He's durned fast in locating us. You'd figger that galoot spent all his time snoopin' around this canyon – never seems to be away.'

The three men stared grimly over the silent floor of the canyon. The first shot had been a drygulch shot with the intention of killing, but the attacker had probably hurried his shot. Certainly the shell had missed Wade. Now that there was no chance of surprise the attacker was silent. Maybe he was working his way to a better vantage point.

Wade stared keenly across at the other canyon wall, which was a broken and jagged line of rocks. Men could hide among that pileup. And a rifle could reach across the canyon with good effect. That wasn't so good when they had only Colts with which to reply.

The next moment, as if in answer to his thoughts, two rifles spoke from the other side of the canyon and dust spat as the slugs bit into the rocks inches from Wade and Tommy. As the angry echoes died away, Wade shouted with grim satisfaction: 'Two o' them!'

'Kinda long range for our hoglegs,' drawled Dave

Latimer. 'Ain't no use wasting lead over that distance.'

'Well, we can't jest sit here behind these rocks!' yelled Tommy.

'Don't yuh move,' warned Wade. 'Those galoots have got the range by now. They're hopin' for one of us to move.'

'Wal, we can't jest sit here,' yelled Tommy indignantly.

Wade glanced sideways at him and smiled. 'Take it easy. I'm going out to hunt the galoots, not you!'

'But —'

'You can cover me with a fusillade of shots,' retorted Wade Tulane. 'I figure that will keep those *hombres* ducking down altho' yuh can't hope to hit at this long range. I want to git up this canyon wall, make a way along the top and git round the dead end. Mebbe I kin get near to those gunslicks and drop them.'

'But you're takin' all the chances,' objected Tommy, staring across the intervening sand at the grim-faced range wanderer.

'I've bin doin' that sort of thing for a long time,' was the crisp answer. 'An' I might get away with it. Now give them *hombres* a hail of lead, Tommy – Dave!'

As the shooting started, Wade Tulane dashed for the jagged canyon wall, flinging a couple of shots across the canyon floor in the hope that they would add to the deterring effect of the hail of lead. He had to use both hands as well as his feet, however, in the next few grim moments. He climbed the canyon wall swiftly, darting through small crevices in the wall, hauling himself up to rough ledges without a pause. The guns below cracked the air. A shot whistled past his head once and dug into the rock, sending chips and dust flying. Then he reached the top and darted into a long crevice which extended for some distance. A few moments later he was well away from danger and bent upon getting round the dead end of the canyon so that he could reach the other canyon wall. He figured to creep up on two galoots and see how they liked some swift Colt lead.

Wade scrambled along the top of the canyon wall, a crouched figure hidden from view. He jumped from rock to rock, dodging the clumps of prickly pear, hoping he would not blunder into a rattler. He rounded the dead end of the canyon and worked his way down the rocky wall in which Rip Heggety and his pal were hidden. That the galoot was Rip Heggety he had no doubt.

Wade went through a slit which was filled with cholla cactus, but it was the only way if he wanted to remain in cover. The spikes tore at his range clothes. He stepped up on to bare rock at the end of the slit and then dropped down into a sort of gully, continuing along the canyon wall like this for about twenty yards.

He heard the exchange of a few shots below. The echoes whipped across the golden sand of the canyon floor. Then the shooting subsided. Dave Latimer and Tommy seemed to be successfully keeping under cover. Then, grimly, he judged he was close to the position from where Rip Heggety and his sidekick were shooting. He would have to exercise care.

Wade inched along and suddenly sank close to the rock, his Colt in his right hand. He saw a head move from behind a boulder below and then dart back again. There was not time for a shot, but this proved he had located the two men.

Grimly, he hoped he had the guts to shoot a man in the back, for that was the momentary view he had got of one of the men. If the chance came again, he would have to trigger for the sake of Tommy Camden and Dave Latimer, who were not gunmen in any way.

Wade slid forward over the bare slab of rock, in order to get another few inches of advantage. He wondered where the men had hidden their horses; probably some way back among the natural corrals made by the rocks. He lay grim and ruthless. So far he had not really identified the men, but he was sure the chief hellion was Rip Heggety. That jasper had sworn to get vengeance on Wade Tulane. Seemed most likely he would end his wild days without it!

Wade heard the sound of his own breathing as he

lay so close to the hot rock, and as he slid forward yet another inch his belt scraped the rock giving him the certain feeling that the other two men down below, among the huddle of boulders, must surely hear him.

But they did not, and then something happened that surprised even Wade Tulane. He heard a shout and then across the silent air of the canyon came the rapid tattoo of thudding hoofs. The sound increased in volume as suddenly as it had arrived. Another shout and then two riders came tearing into the canyon.

Wade raised himself, narrowed his eyes. He saw instantly that the first rider was a girl – Stella Camden! She was followed by the hardy figure of Bill Hapner.

Even as Wade raised himself, he sensed movement among the two men below him. A man jumped to a boulder and drew his rifle on the two swiftly-moving riders.

Wade just had time to realize that this galoot was not Rip Heggety and then he triggered his Colt down at the rannigan.

One shot and the man plunged forward, his rifle falling from his grasp. The Colt slug echoed away. As it faded, Wade heard the rasp of boots on loose rock chips and he knew Rip Heggety was making an escape. The other man was dead, sure thing. Grimly, he felt some satisfaction in eliminating the sidekick from the scene, then he scrambled to his feet, and, crouching, went forward among the rocky debris on the top of the canyon wall.

That he had saved Stella Camden from a death-shot he was certain. But he wished he had killed Rip Heggety. Wade Tulane saw the galoot momentarily as he chased after him. As he saw him, he fired. The slug apparently missed which was not surprising in a chase. Then Rip Heggety loosened off a couple of shots which forced Wade to duck behind the nearest rock. A second later and he poked out an arm and fired at the hellion.

Rip Heggety was not hurt. He dashed out of cover and flung himself down a crevice between the rock. Wade heard the crashing sound of his progress as boots slithered on loose rock chips and crunched against cholla cactus.

Wade went forward grimly and without wasting any time, because he wanted to get a bead on this man. But too much rashness could easily be danger-ous. Rip Heggety's guns were equally as dangerous as Wade's!

It was a grim game of chase among the never-ending spread of broken rocks, with swift slugs bark-ing every so often. Then Wade had his stroke of bad luck. He slipped badly and fell, striking the side of his head against a protruding knob of rock. He lay dazed for some valuable seconds during which time Rip Heggety made his getaway, not realizing for a moment that his enemy was, in fact, temporarily helpless.

Wade Tulane rose to his feet, stared grimly ahead and then holstered his gun. He knew that Rip Heggety had got that all-important headstart. He couldn't see the man, nor could he hear him.

Wade went on, slowly at first, for a few more minutes, moving carefully through the jagged rocky debris. Then he heard the sound of a horse's hoofs making that clattering noise on loose rock chips and knew that Rip Heggety was making his getaway. Wade broke into a run, leaping from rock to rock. But the horse evidently had a way out of this chaotic pileup of volcanic rock for the sound of hoofs faded away. It seemed there a defile leading away to smoother ground. Wade halted and then turned. Rip Heggety was lighting out but most probably only to fight another day!

Wade returned to the spot where he had shot down Rip Heggety's sidekick. He descended into the boulder strewn hole and examined the man. One of the ruffian placer miners, he guessed. Well, the man was dead.

Quickly he piled small boulders over the body, and then picked up the man's rifle. Wade stared down at the canyon wall, discovering a rather tricky path down to the canyon floor. He started on the task of climbing down.

A bit later he walked steadily across the yellow sands of the canyon floor, on a straight line for the others at the other side. They waited for him, a small bunch of people still warily holding guns. Wade strode up, his boots crunching harshly against the hard, sun-baked sand.

'One dead,' he said curtly and nodded to the sheriff. Then he caught Stella's eyes and a smile came into his bleak eyes. 'Guess I don't know what yuh're doin' here – an' with the sheriff!'

'I found that you were in danger,' she said swiftly. 'Leo Sand came into the store to bother me and I knew by his words that something bad was planned for you.'

'Leo Sand!' reflected Wade. 'I might teach him not to bother you. What did he do – or say?'

Stella lightly touched his arm. 'What does it matter – you're safe!' She turned. 'All of you, thank goodness.'

Sheriff Hapner turned and surveyed the work the three men had done towards uncovering the old cave.

'So this is the reason for all the durned grief. Gold! I might ha' know it. So William Camden died because of this!'

'Yep, this is what Rip Heggety and his brothers were after,' snapped Wade Tulane. 'According to a map William Camden left hidden under the floor-board of his house, there should be gold hidden in this cave – but not the stuff the miners dig out. Nope! This is old gold, cached by the Siomi Indians.'

'Yep, Miss Stella told me a lot about on the ride down,' said Sheriff Hapner.

'Yuh nearly rode into a drygulch,' commented Wade dryly.

Bill Hapner grimaced. 'Guess I let Miss Stella have too much rope! She went dashing ahead an' I had to follow.'

'We tried to warn them about those two galoots hiding with the rifle,' added Tommy, 'but I reckon Stella and the sheriff didn't understand our shouts.'

'How about getting on with the work now, Wade?' called out Tommy Camden eagerly.

'Wal, we're sticking around now until we locate that gold – or otherwise,' agreed Wade. 'I reckon Rip Heggety will find another sidekick if he jest mentions gold.'

'You mean we can't leave the site,' asked Dave Latimer.

Wade was finding time to roll a cigarette. 'Looks that way. We'll have to stick hyar until we git this settled.'

Sheriff Hapner scratched his head and pushed his Stetson back again to keep the strong sun out of his eyes.

'Guess I'll have to ride back to town. But you kin rely on me to say nothin' about this gold until yuh got it out. By then I guess the story will git around the town. Yuh can't keep news o' gold a secret fer very long.'

'We'll get the gold out if we can,' snapped Dave Latimer. 'Not that I'm interested because my ranch satisfies me. But maybe Stella and Tommy might use gold to fix them up in this life.'

'How about you, Tulane?' questioned the sheriff. 'What d'yuh feel about gold?'

'Me?' Wade inhaled his cigarette. 'It's useful stuff iffen a man uses it right. I ain't sayin' any more except that this gold don't belong to me.'

'Fair enough,' rapped the sheriff. 'Wal, anybody ridin' back to town with me?' And he looked directly at the girl.

'You ought to go back,' said Tommy slowly.

'And be pestered by Leo Sand?' flashed the girl.

'You could stay with the Grahams – they're good friends of ours. Mac Graham would smash Leo Sand if you said the word. You'd better git back to town, Stella.'

'Not me!' flashed the girl and she gripped the headstall of her horse all the firmer. 'I'm staying right here until I see that gold.'

Tommy glanced at the sinking sun.

'Might be all night, sis!' he protested.

'I don't care,' she rejoined. 'I've got a saddle blanket and the sand is warm.'

'But what if Rip Heggety returns with a pal?' put in Wade Tulane.

'There'll be four of us,' replied Stella sweetly. 'And I noticed you've got the dead man's rifle.'

'Gosh, you're stubborn!' exploded Tommy.

'Just like you, my dear,' said Stella gently. 'I note you're using that injured arm – how stubborn are you?'

And that was the way Stella Camden influenced the others into allowing her to stay with them in the canyon. The sheriff rode away, shaking his head, a man with other problems because he had to keep law and order in Laredo and could not concern himself entirely with the affairs of Tommy and Stella.

The girl rounded up the horses that had strayed during the shooting and tethered them near to some dried grass. Wasting no more of the evening sun, Wade, Tommy and Dave Latimer set to work again on the hard task of clearing a way into the old Siomi cave. They had no real idea of how much work would be needed to excavate the opening into the cave. They just had to toil on grimly, hoping the fall that had blocked and concealed the cave for more than a century did not extend too far into the actual natural cave.

Now and then, during a spell from the hard graft,

Wade Tulane would stride around in a circle from the site in order to search the canyon – and the heaped rocks – for sign of strangers. At first he did not expect Rip Heggety to return to the scene so quickly, but later he felt sure the hellion would drift up.

It was Stella's task to maintain a lookout as well. Wade stood beside her for a moment.

'He'll be back,' he said.

'He's a – a – devil!' she breathed. 'He knew Dad had the secret to this gold and for a long time he's been determined to get it. I reckon he – he – won't stop now.'

10

THE BAD DEAL

Wade Tulane and the other two men worked inces-
santly, pulling the rocks out of the cave mouth and
piling them to the rear. This process built up a sort of
rampart around the area, something that might be
useful if Rip Heggety or, in fact, any other ruffian
decided to get curious about the cave. But the hard
work told on Tommy Camden; he wasn't used to it
and his arm was still painful. As the sun sank lower
and there was still no sign of the actual cave, he
broke off work at Wade's order and joined Stella in
her position as lookout.

'Better make some grub, sis,' he murmured. 'The
others are famished. I'll help you gather some tinder.
Won't make any difference about a fire showing
because Rip Heggety knows where to find us if he
wants to start anything.'

'How is the work going?' she asked.

'Fine. I think we'll burst into the cave pretty soon – but I think the sun will sink first.'

'Then there'll be no light in which to work.'

'Guess not. Seems mighty likely we'll have to break into the actual cave at sun-up.'

'Sometimes I wonder if gold is worth all this,' she muttered.

'We can't leave it for a devil like Rip Heggety to pick up, sis!'

'I guess not. And if he killed Daddy justice should be done about that, too!' she said with sudden fierceness. She went to Tommy's horse and untied the food bag. When the three men had set off they had anticipated the need for food and they had coffee and beans, water and two pans and enamel mugs. Stella set up the fire with the aid of some stones. Then, glancing at Wade and Dave Latimer, still toiling in the failing light, she went out of the stockade with Tommy and searched for dry tinder.

This was mostly dead cactus root and greasewood which they found mostly in odd nooks under the wall of the canyon.

Stella went along with Tommy, but somehow she found herself a fair distance away from him. And then Tommy Camden made the mistake of returning with his armful of dry tinder and stacking it near the fireplace.

Stella was not actually aware that she was alone and some distance from the cave. She was busy picking up tinder when she sensed the movement on her left side. She wheeled around, her mouth opening in shock. But her scream was a tiny thing that was choked off for the man leaped at her and clamped a huge palm over her mouth.

Her struggles availed her little. She was immediately dragged back to the rocky hideout, there to be greeted by another man – Rip Heggety, no less!

'Not another struggle outa yuh, my beauty!' grated the hellion. 'Come on, Sep – let's move back. I reckon we got a prize worth holdin' on to. Right now we're too close up to them rannigans if we want to hold this gal.'

The man known as Sep Corry, an unshaven ruffian without much brain, nodded and, gripping the girl cruelly, hauled her back along the rocky crevice they had used in order to get close to the cave. Quickly, in spite of the burden of a struggling girl, they went right back along the canyon wall to the cunning hole where they had hidden the horses. It was a recess that could be overlooked a hundred times by searching men.

'Hold her, Sep! I'll tie her,' snarled Rip Heggety, and he got the rope from his saddle and rapidly cut lengths with which he bound the girl. He tore his red bandanna and made a sound gag; this he used to

147

prevent Stella from screaming the moment Sep Corry's hand was withdrawn.

'Got her!' Rip exulted. 'Now maybe we kin use this gal as a trick card!'

'What's the use o' this, Heggety?' asked Sep stupidly.

The other laughed. 'Yuh'll see. Maybe this gal is a good swap for a cache of gold – who knows! That's what those galoots are after, Sep. Gold! Old Injun gold! I knew it, but I never could figure where the place was in this canyon!'

'I ain't ever heerd o' Injun gold, Heggety.'

'Yuh a dumb cluck,' stated Rip. 'But no matter. This gold is buried in the canyon wall – a cave, I guess. Old man Camden had the secret, damn him. But he wouldn't talk and he got his slug in the back. Maybe that was a bad play, because Mac and me never could find the plan showing the location of the Injun cave.'

Stella's eyes flashed with hatred for this ruffian. She was gagged and bound but she could hear!

'Mac an' me knew Camden got the secret of this Injun gold off an old Injun who said he was a member of the old Siomi tribe. This Injun was dyin' when he told Camden the secret. I guess that durned draper made a drawin' of the location, but me and Mac never found it, although we figgered to buy the store. The blamed fools refused so we ransacked the

148

place. Still no use. Aw, well, we're on to it now, Sep!'
And Rip Heggety gave a hearty chuckle.

'Let's git along to them fellers!' slurred Sep Corry.
'I reckon we could kill them mighty fast.'

'That's alluz yore way o' thinking,' snapped Rip
Heggety. 'Those cusses ain't so easy, Sep. But I'd sure
like to see some of em' dead – partic'ly that ornery
Tulane! He's crossed me too many times.'

'Let's git alawng!' snarled the other. 'Hell, there's
only one way to git gold and thet's to shoot for it.'

'Right,' decided Rip. 'We'll mosey along again to
the point in the rocks. But leave things to me, yuh
understand? Maybe we'll shoot an' maybe we'll make
a lil deal with the gal. Yuh jest take orders, Sep.' The
other nodded. Rip Heggety glanced at him in the
darkening night and sneered. If Sep was useful for a
shooting affray, so much the better. If he got himself
killed, then that was too bad!

Rip Heggety thought that Sep Corry might get
killed sooner or later because gold was too valuable
to split two ways.

Leaving the girl in the hidden nook, the two ruffi-
ans set off again along the trail back to the advantage
point. The night darkened with the suddenness of
these parts. This was to the good for Sep Corry and
Rip Heggety. They reached the last possible stand
among the rocks along the side of the canyon wall
and sank to the ground and conferred in whispers.

'Remember – yuh take orders!'

'Shore. I kin see a feller – yuh want I should shoot now?'

'Nope. What the hell's the use o' killin' one? Jest wait, Sep. Maybe we kin get the bead on the three o' them.'

'Can't hear any sounds of those sidewinders workin',' grunted Sep Corry.

That was true and there was a good reason for the lack of noise.

By now Tommy had realized that Stella was missing. He had gasped out the news to Wade and Dave Latimer. Wade had spent some minutes walking around in the gloom, the rifle held at the waist ready to plug the first stranger he encountered. Wade had gone some way along the canyon, searching the thousands of nooks and crannies but to no effect. He stared at the eerie shapes of giant fallen boulders that had lain at the foot of the canyon wall for centuries. The boulders were rounded and smooth, the result of hundreds of years of scouring winds and sandstorms. The rocks lay in grotesque heaps, sometimes like sentinels in the night. A man could hide in a thousand holes.

With the light faint and gloomy it was a hopeless task looking for the girl – and yet Wade ached to find her. He just had to find her. And he realized Stella had not just got lost! Something grim had happened.

She was being detained. Rip Heggety was around.

Warily, he backed, rifle in hand, making a way back to the camp where Tommy and Dave Latimer waited with guns in hands, eyes searching the dark night.

'No good!' he snapped. 'I jest can't sight anyone.'

'I shouldn't have allowed her out o' my sight!' groaned Tommy.

'She couldn't jest get lost,' commented Dave Latimer grimly.

'That means Rip Heggety,' muttered Tommy. 'Gawd, I'm not a gunman but I'd like to kill that man!'

'Yuh might have a chance,' grated Wade. 'There'll be a play afore long. Wish I knew where they were!'

The three men stood in the gap of the barricade and the night sky lightened a bit with a hint of a rising moon. Wade and Dave Latimer walked out of the rampart of rocks which they had rolled out of the cave mouth, and they took slow strides down the canyon, pausing every few yards to stare around in the hope that they might see something that moved.

It was then that Sep Corry fired, getting a dim idea that Rip Heggety had given the order.

The gun lanced flame from out of the darkness and the slug took away Dave Latimer's hat.

Wade and the rancher dropped flat to the desert and tried to emulate burrowing animals. They hugged

151

the earth. A cloud sailed over the light patch of sky and the canyon was momentarily darkened again.

Running for the comparative shelter of two lone boulders, Wade and the rancher loosened off fast shots at the place where they had seen the gunflame. Immediately more shots flared out and the slugs spat into the hard sand around Wade and Dave Latimer.

Wade waited for the moonlight to appear again. He hugged the small boulder, his hand only poking out and holding his six-shooter. He had the rifle by his side. He was not discarding it. But the Colt would serve if only he could get a bead on the attackers.

It was then that Sep Corry made another dim-witted mistake. As the cloud floated away and the sky lightened, the ruffian rose from behind a rock and aimed his gun at the boulder sheltering Wade Tulane.

Wade snapped off a lightning shot that took the man right between the eyes. The man staggered out of his hiding place; quite visible to Wade and Dave Latimer. Then Sep Corry fell forward like a felled tree and lay absolutely still, arms splayed out.

There was an angry shout from Rip Heggety. 'Damn yuh, Tulane! Keep that hogleg holstered from now on! I've got the girl! Iffen yuh want to see her alive again, git back to thet cave and start working.'

'What do yuh mean?'

'I mean I want thet gold! Remember I got the girl. I'll make a deal with yuh. Git back and work on that cave – uncover thet gold and then clear out. I'll hand yuh the Camden girl.'

'That's some deal!' mocked Wade. 'You reckon to make us work, huh!'

'I know yuh ain't got the gold uncovered!' shouted the other. 'But there's all night. Yuh kin build a fire and git to work. I'll be watchin' yuh.'

'Maybe yuh'd like to come forward an' lend a hand?' shouted Dave Latimer.

'No sirree! Not unless you galoots figger to throw down yore guns. Yuh c'd do thet. I'll settle for either deal.' And there was a triumphant laugh from Rip Heggety as he considered the alternative. 'Remember, I got the gal and iffen yuh figger to trick me or refuse a deal I kin blast her with one shot.'

'We might blast you!' shouted Wade.

'Thet would be too bad, mister. The gal might die of starvation iffen she wasn't found – and I reckon she's well-hidden. Yep, she would jest lie in that hole and rot if yuh *hombres* eliminated me. So don't git too gun-handy.'

Silence fell over the scene for what seemed a long time. Then Wade Tulane spoke harshly.

'All right, Heggety, we'll git back to workin' on the cave. Maybe we're near to uncovering the hidden gold – I don't know. We'll make the deal as soon as we break into the cave. You'll hand over Miss Stella safe and sound. That suit yuh?'

'Yep – unless yuh want to throw down yore guns. I c'd join yuh if you'd do that.'

'We don't need help,' snapped Wade. 'All right, git the work started.'

'Shore – if yuh beat it. We don't want to be plugged in the back.'

Another laugh rose from the dark rocks. 'All right. I reckon yuh know what'll happen to the gal iffen yuh try any tricks. I'm movin' back, Tulane – an' if yuh try to plug me remember the gal might jest lie and rot.'

Wade lay flat behind his boulder, signalling Dave Latimer to do the same, and waited. He heard the sound of boots on loose rubble but he did not see any sign of Rip Heggety. The man was hiding himself well even if he did hold a trump card in the fact that Stella's life could not be risked.

Wade gave Rip Heggety a few minutes and then he ran across the canyon floor at a crouch, making for the cave site. No shots came his way. Presently, Dave Latimer joined him.

'Have we got to work for thet ornery devil?' raged the rancher.

'We'll make a play of doing some work,' snapped Wade. 'I figgered this was the best move – better than dropping our guns.'

'Shore – better than thet. But, Wade, how can we best that devil? Yuh got an idea – I figger yuh have, man!'

154

Tommy Camden joined them. 'I heard the shootin'. Didn't seem anything I could do.'

Wade slapped him on his good shoulder. 'Never rush out where there's shooting. Yuh heard Heggety?'

'Yeah, every word.'

'He's got Miss Stella hidden away someplace. He's right – we might never find her if he got killed.' Wade stared grimly at the young fellow. 'Set to work, amigos. That snake has got to think we're workin' on the Injun cave.'

'You got an idea?'

'Sure. Rip Heggety can't keep tag on us all the time. Even if he's watchin' us work, this is still touch-and-go for him, too. I'm going out to track him down. But not just yet. We've got to make some noise just so that he'll figger we're keepin' to the deal. After awhile I'll slip out —'

And that was the way they worked it. They pitched into some work, the three of them, and pulled the boulder back and made a lot of noise in one way or another. Then Wade, figuring that the light was too poor for the hidden Rip Heggety to see everything, crept out, concealing himself in the nearest cranny. He spent about thirty seconds there and then moved on, carefully because he didn't want to give a hint to the hidden man, if he was watching, that some trick was about to be played.

Wade knew the dangers, not that he was thinking

about himself. He was thinking about the girl. Just to realize that she was in great danger sharpened his knowledge that he was in love with her. He, the man who had lived hard, felt a startling surge of love for this girl. And God help the man who harmed her!

He was out to get Rip Heggety for good – and that meant death. But he could not shoot the man even if he sighted him because he wanted the location of the hidden girl.

Wade Tulane crept into another crevice of which there were plenty, and in this manner got some distance from the site of the cave. He looked back. He saw the dark figures of Tommy and Dave as they moved among the deeper shadows thrown by huge boulders. If this was what Rip Heggety was watching, then it was hardly possible for the rannigan to keep exact check on the men. At the best Tommy and Dave were mostly fleeting shapes in the night.

Wade Tulane crept to a biggish boulder and then looked around him in a concentrated effort to locate Rip Heggety. The man must be somewhere in a ring around the cave site. He was obviously behind some of the volcanic rocks. He could not be lying on the flat floor of the canyon, although it was possible in the darkness.

Wade put his hands to his mouth and made a low howling noise like a prowling hyena baying at the moon. He waited, staring keenly all around him.

Almost immediately a harsh voice snarled an oath and a stone whizzed through the air.

Wade grinned. So somebody was trying to scare away the banshee hyena!

He blessed the good fortune that had prompted him to think of the hyena trick. It was an old Indian ruse and befitted this dark silent canyon with its legends of ancient Indian tribes.

He had noted the spot where from the curse and the stone had come. He let the silence of the night fall around him for a little while and then he began to slide forward on his belly. He moved quietly, making less noise than a snake.

After a minute of going in the direction of the curse, he became aware of the man lying flat behind the medium sized boulder. This must be Rip Heggety, keeping his cunning watch on the Indian cave site.

The man was lying flat on his stomach, his hat level with the top of the boulder, watching. Wade came up so quietly the other man never realised what was happening. He seemed to have no suspicion that one of the men from the cave site was missing.

Wade knew he could not bring out a gun and shoot the man dead. That way there was great danger that Stella would perish somewhere among the chaos of jumbled boulders that formed the canyon. That was an unthinkable fate!

But if Wade could not shoot Rip Heggety, that man was not bound by any such considerations towards Wade! If the hellion suspected he was being stalked, out would come his gun!

It was a good thing that Heggety was intent upon the men working at clearing the cave mouth, for Wade was sure he made some slight sounds. But they were undetected by the other man.

And then it was possible for Wade Tulane to leap to the man's back. He flew through the air and landed with a tremendous wallop on Rip Heggety's back. The man, warned at the last split-second as was inevitable, tried to draw a gun but it never got clear of leather.

Wade smashed a left and right into the man's face. Then Heggety tried to bring his knee up into Wade's guts. Wade rolled and jabbed viciously at Rip Heggety's chin. But this didn't seem to be doing much good. The man was hard as iron.

It wasn't the time for nice behaviour; too many grim things were at stake. Wade shoved a hand down for his gun and brought it out. He still had the advantage in that he was straddling the other man. Wade rammed the butt at the side of Heggety's head. This brought a hideous gasp from the man. He sank.

But a bit later he was full of fight, hissing and uttering threats. Wade rammed the gun butt at the man's head again and this dazed him.

'Git up!' snarled Wade. 'Take me to Miss Stella. I'll gunwhip yuh every time yuh show fight! In fact, I'll gunwhip yuh every ten yards iffen I figger yuh need it. Now move it! I want to find the girl pronto!'

As Rip Heggety staggered to his feet, Wade plucked the six-shooter from the man's holster. 'Git going.'

The hellion staggered along, the fight drained from him. Blood seeped from cuts in his scalp. He was dazed.

But such was his bull-like nature he tried to make a play a few moments later. Wade was ready as the man jerked. The gun butt whipped and nearly felled the *hombre*. With a horrible gasp, Rip Heggety staggered along.

'Don't try it again, feller!' rasped Wade.

But the fight was out of the man. It was impossible for him to take that ruthless punishment. He staggered along, climbed the rocky pileup and showed Wade the great hole where the girl lay bound and gagged.

Wade felled the man, banking on getting him before he recovered his senses. With a leap Wade was beside the girl. His knife cut the bonds and his fingers gently untied the gag.

'Stella – my dear —' He had difficulty in finding the right words. Then she fell into his embrace and he knew everything would be all right, for him and for Stella. The gold would be found and claimed. And Rip Heggety would be tried for his crimes. Leo Sand, too, would face a charge of assault if he ever showed his face in town again.

Wade picked the girl up and carried her to the canyon floor and then gave a great shout that brought Tommy and Dave.

'I've got Stella! And Rip Heggety!'

They ran along, Dave finding time to pick up a length of dried tinder which he lighted at the fire. Rip Heggety was secured and his wrists bound. As for Stella, she was overjoyed at being found. And a special kind of happiness glowed in her eyes whenever she glanced at Wade Tulane.

He knew that he could clear himself of the Wanted charge if he really tried. He had so far run away. But now he would get the stupid business cleared up. It would have to be cleared up for Stella's sake.

'The end of the trail,' he laughed. 'You'll find the gold.'

'We've deserved it,' she smiled.

'Do good by it,' chuckled Dave Latimer.

Tommy Camden grinned. 'You bet! We've got roots in this town and we want to see it grow into something good – and I've a notion Wade will be right there with us from now on!'